P.

# Dashing Through the Snow

# Dashing Through the Snow

## MARY HIGGINS CLARK

## CAROL HIGGINS CLARK

SIMON &
SCHUSTER

London · New York · Sydney · Toronto

A CBS COMPANY

First published in the US by Simon & Schuster, Inc., 2008
First published in Great Britain by Simon & Schuster UK Ltd, 2008
A CBS COMPANY

1 3 5 7 9 10 8 6 4 2

Simon & Schuster UK Ltd
1st Floor, 222 Gray's Inn Road
London WC1X 8HB

www.simonsays.co.uk

Simon & Schuster Australia
Sydney

A CIP catalogue record for this book is available from the British Library

ISBN 978-1-84737-526-1

# Acknowledgments

Once again the tale has been told and once again we enjoyed the experience of writing about our favorite characters, Alvirah and Willy Meehan, Regan and Jack Reilly, and their new friends in Branscombe.

It is our pleasure and joy to thank the people who accompanied us as we were dashing through the snow, our editors, Michael V. Korda and Roz Lippel; our publicist, Lisl Cade; Associate Director of Copyediting Gypsy da Silva; Jacket Designer, Jackie Seow; and Literary Agent, Esther Newberg.

Sleigh bells ring for our family and friends who are always there to cheer us on, particularly "Spouse Extraordinaire" John Conheeney, Irene Clark, Agnes Newton, and Nadine Petry.

To all of these and to our readers, Happy Holidays.

*For Lisl Cade*
*Cherished friend and dedicated publicist*
*With love*

# 1

## *Thursday, December 11th*

In the picturesque town of Branscombe, in the heart of the Granite State of New Hampshire, lights and banners were being strung to herald the first, and many hoped annual, Festival of Joy. It was the second week of December, and the town was buzzing. Volunteers, their faces glowing with good will, were helping to transform the village green into a holiday wonderland. The weather was even cooperating. As if on cue, a light snow was falling. The pond was frozen solid, ready for the ice-skating events planned for the weekend. Most everyone in Branscombe grew up on ice skates.

Learning of the Festival and its purpose to promote the wholesome lifestyle of a small town and the true meaning of the holiday season, a major cable network, BUZ, had decided to cover the event. They had big plans for a warmhearted special that would air on Christmas Eve.

Muffy Patton, the thirty-year-old wife of the newly elected mayor, had suggested the concept of the Festival at a summer meeting of the town council. "It's time for us to do something special for this town. Other towns in our state are famous for their sled races and bike weeks. Branscombe has been ignored for too long. We should celebrate the fact that Branscombe is a simple hamlet, full of people with good old-fashioned values. There's no better place to raise a family."

Her husband, Steve, had agreed heartily. The third-generation owner of a real estate business, he was all for promoting the land values in the area. His firm had houses listed for sale that would be perfect as a country retreat for people living in Boston. A persuasive and spirited idea man, Steve had helped Muffy generate rousing enthusiasm for the Festival.

"In so many places the spirit of Christmas isn't what it used to be," he opined. "It's all about shopping days and sales. Artificial Christmas trees jamming the stores before the Halloween pumpkins have disappeared. My city friends tell me they all get short-tempered and sulky with the stress of the season. Let's have ourselves a down-home weekend, with caroling in the town square, a new set of lights for the big tree, and lots of fun stuff to do all weekend. We'll set the example that Christmas 'tis the season to be jolly and joyful."

"What about food?" one of the council members asked practically.

"We'll get Conklin's to cater the whole works. We'll price

tickets just to cover our costs. We're so lucky to have a family-owned store like that in this town—it's an institution."

They had all nodded, thinking of how soothing it felt to just walk into Conklin's. The scents of roasting turkeys, baking hams, simmering pasta sauces, and bubbling chocolate chip cookies were a treat to inhale. Food fit for a king, and a few aisles down you'd find wrenches and garden hoses and even clothespins. People in Branscombe liked their sheets and towels to smell of fresh, cold air.

By the end of the meeting, the enthusiasm had spread to a fever pitch. Now, three months later, the Festival would begin the next day. The opening ceremony was scheduled for Friday at 5 P.M. in the town square. Branscombe's huge Christmas tree had already been lit. All the other trees along Main Street and around the Bowling Green would go on at exactly the same moment as Santa arrived on his horse-drawn sleigh. Candles were to be distributed, and the church choir would lead the crowd in singing Christmas carols. A buffet supper in the church basement would be followed by the first of many screenings of *It's a Wonderful Life*.

On Saturday, Nora Regan Reilly, whose son-in-law was a close college friend of the mayor, would be signing her just-published book during the holiday bazaar. She had also agreed to hold a story hour with the children. Outside, there would be hay rides and sleigh rides, and ice skaters would be serenaded by recordings of Bing Crosby and Frank Sinatra singing everyone's favorite Christmas music. Saturday night another buffet supper would be followed by a staging of "A Christmas Carol," performed by the amateur Branscombe thespian group. Sunday morning the festivities would wrap up with a pancake breakfast, yet another meal to be held in the church basement.

So far all the plans were running smoothly.

Over at Conklin's Market, the employees were working non-stop to prepare for the weekend. The Festival had been a great idea for the town and for Conklin's business, but the workers were worn out. The holiday season, from Thanksgiving through New Year's Day, was always busy, but this year things were crazed. And thanks to the television coverage, more and more people from the surrounding towns were expected to join in the activities. The workers at Conklin's had to be ready to supply extra food at a moment's notice. They knew they wouldn't be able to enjoy a single minute of the festivities themselves, but they were sure that Mr. Conklin would reward them with a bigger bonus than usual, a bonus that traditionally had been handed out by now. Some of the staff had even been grumbling that they hadn't received it yet.

Tonight the 8:00 closing hour couldn't come fast

enough for any of them. At ten of eight, Glenda, the head cashier, was locking up one of the registers when the front door flew open and Mr. Conklin's bossy new wife, Rhoda, marched in, followed by her increasingly sheepish husband, Sam, whom she now referred to as Samuel. In her late fifties, Rhoda and old man Conklin had met at a senior singles dance in Boston, when he was visiting his son for the weekend. It didn't take Rhoda long to realize that Sam was ripe for the picking. A recent widower, he didn't know what hit him until one day he found himself in his best blue suit, a flower in his lapel, and the sight of Rhoda in a glittery cocktail dress, marching down the aisle toward him. Since then life at Conklin's Market had not been the same. Rhoda was trying to put her stamp on a forty-year-old business that had run just fine without her.

She told Ralph the butcher, whose roasted turkeys were legendary, that he was using too much butter when he basted them. Her attempt to convince the sweet-faced, seventy-five-year-old Marion, who had run the bakery department since Day One, to use canned fillers for her cakes and pies, was not well received. Tommy, a burly, ruggedly handsome young man in his twenties, who had a magical way with salads and sandwiches, was told to cut down on the generous portions of cold cuts he allotted to the submarine sandwiches. Duncan, the head of produce, was mortally offended when Rhoda retrieved a bruised apple he'd tossed out and put it back in the bin.

And then there was Glenda. Glenda knew, because she handled the cold, hard cash, that whenever Rhoda was around she was being watched like a hawk. This offended Glenda to the core. She had worked at Conklin's since high school, and in the sixteen years following there'd never been a dime missing on her watch, nor would there ever be. Now the sight of the new Mrs. Conklin made Glenda's stomach churn. While the employees had all been working themselves to death, Rhoda had obviously been out having her hair done. The broad white streak that ran from her forehead to the back of her midnight black hair looked freshly oiled. Thanks to Glenda's referring to that dye job as "reskunked," Rhoda was now known to the employees of Conklin's as "The Skunk."

Rhoda darted over to Glenda. "Wait till you see the surprise we have for our five key employees! Samuel and I would like you, Ralph, Marion, Duncan, and Tommy to come to the office as soon as you're finished closing up."

"Sure," Glenda answered, as she suspiciously eyed the two heavy shopping bags with the logo of the local frame shop that Mr. Conklin was carrying. What could be in them?

Ten minutes later she found out. The group stood together as Rhoda made her little speech about how the Festival of Joy was really bringing home the true meaning of the holidays. "Samuel and I are so pleased that the town of Branscombe is being celebrated for its emphasis on people, rather than things. Spirituality. Good neighbors. That's why we've decided, in lieu of a cash bonus, which is so mercenary, to give you something else." Diving into the bags, she began to hand each of them a gift-wrapped package. "Open them all at once so it doesn't ruin the surprise for any of you."

A dead silence fell over the room as the senior employees of Conklin's, after yanking the string and paper off the boxes, found themselves staring at the group picture of the five of them taken with the bride and groom six months ago on the porch of the Branscombe Inn. The frames were engraved with the words, "In appreciation of your long and faithful service. Joyous holidays to you! Samuel and Rhoda Conklin."

Glenda was appalled. Every one of us needs a cash bonus and was counting on it, she thought angrily. Duncan had gotten so thrifty he didn't even go in our group lottery tickets today. She was planning to use her bonus to pay off the cash advance she'd taken on her credit card. She'd needed the money to reimburse her ex-husband, Harvey, for his clothes that were "maliciously ruined" when she left them out in two garbage bags on the driveway, just as an unexpected storm made its appearance. Violent winds had blown the bags into the street just as a delivery truck rumbled through. Five minutes late, Harvey found his clothes scattered all over the street, soaked and squashed.

"If I hadn't left them out at the appointed time," Glenda

had protested, "he'd be complaining I was in contempt of court."

The judge didn't buy it and ordered her to pay the replacement value of the tacky getups Harvey favored. The bonus would have meant she could have paid him off and be rid of him and his cheating ways forever.

"You don't have to thank us," Rhoda chirped, as they all held the pictures in their hands. "Come along, Samuel. We need to get a good night's rest. It's going to be a busy weekend."

Mr. Conklin followed her out the door without making eye contact with any of his workers.

Glenda saw that Marion was blinking back tears. "I promised my grandson a nice wedding present," she said. "But after paying for the flight to California, now I don't know what I'll be able to afford . . ."

Ralph moaned, "Judy and I were planning to take a cruise this winter to give ourselves a break. With both girls in college, we're always stretched to the limit. Even tonight Judy is babysitting to pick up some extra cash."

Tommy looked as though steam was about to come out of his ears. Glenda knew that he still lived with his elderly parents because they needed his help financially. A good skier, he'd been planning to take a long overdue trip out west with some of his pals.

Tall, thin, quiet Duncan, who at almost thirty-two was just a couple of years younger than Glenda, grabbed his coat and

---

thrust his arms into it. As he pulled up the hood, his sandy hair fell forward on his forehead. His face was flushed. Glenda had always had an almost maternal feeling for him. He was so methodical, so orderly, his produce section of Conklin's was always so inviting, that it was out of character for him to be visibly upset. "I'm out of here," he said, his voice shaking.

Glenda caught his arm. "Wait a minute," she urged. "Why don't we all go down to Salty's Tavern and get a bite to eat?"

Duncan looked at her as though she was nuts. "And spend more money that we don't have?" he asked, his voice rising with every word. "The financial planning course I've been taking emphasizes that eating out when you can just as easily fix something at home is one of the primary reasons so many people are in debt."

"Then go home and make yourself a peanut butter sandwich," Glenda snapped. "Don't you think we're all upset? Sometimes after a blow like this it's good to get out with friends and relax."

But Duncan was gone before she could finish.

"*Some* misery loves company," Ralph shrugged with an attempt at a smile. "Let's go."

"I'm with you," Marion cried. "I almost never touch the stuff, but right now I could use a stiff drink."

\* \* \*

Two hours later, Glenda, Tommy, Ralph, and Marion, feeling somewhat better, and even able to joke about The Skunk, were about to leave Salty's Tavern when Tommy pointed to the television over the bar.

They all watched as the local announcer, his voice excited, cried, "There are two winners in the mega-mega multistate lottery tonight. Two winners who will share 360 million dollars, and what is so incredible is that both tickets were bought within ten miles of one another in New Hampshire!"

As one, their bodies froze. Could they even dare hope that their group could possibly have one of the winning tickets? For every drawing, they each threw in a dollar and purchased five tickets. They played the same five numbers on each ticket and the same separate Powerball numbers on four of them, but the fifth Powerball number they took turns choosing.

The announcer read the first five numbers. "They're ours!" Marion shrieked.

"And the Powerball number is . . . 32!"

Tommy and Ralph pounded the table. "No!" they cried. "32 isn't one of our regular Powerball numbers."

"What about the extra number this week?" Marion cried. "It was Duncan's turn, but he decided not to play."

Glenda was digging in her purse. Her hands were trembling. Sweat popped out on her forehead. She pulled out her wallet and unzipped the special compartment where she kept the tickets.

"Duncan told me the Powerball number he had chosen. He was about to hand me his dollar, then put it back in his wallet. I was so used to buying five tickets that when I got to the convenience store and pulled out a five dollar bill, I thought what the heck? I bought the extra ticket and used Duncan's Powerball number . . . I'm sure it was in the 30s."

"I can't take it," Marion cried. "What was it? Hurry up Glenda!" she croaked.

Glenda dealt out the tickets like a deck of cards. "Let's all take a look."

In the dim light of the votive candle, the tickets were hard to read. Marion bent over, straining to decipher the Powerball number on the ticket in front of her. An other-worldly grunting sound emanated from the depths of her being. "Oh, my God!" she finally screamed as she jumped up, waving the ticket. "WE WON! WE WON!"

"Are you SURE it's 32?" Glenda shouted.

Marion's hand was shaking so much the ticket fluttered to the floor. Tommy reached down and grabbed it. "It's got the number 32!" he boomed. "It's 32!"

By now, everyone in the tavern was on his feet.

"The four of us get to split 180 million bucks!" he shouted as he lifted the diminutive Marion off her feet and spun her around.

Wait till Harvey hears about this, Glenda thought wildly as she and Ralph hugged.

"How about one of those group hugs?" Marion cried as the four of them put their arms around each other, laughing, crying, and still not believing.

This can't be true, Glenda thought. How can it possibly be true? Our lives have changed forever.

"Drinks for everyone," the bartender cried. "But you guys are paying!"

The foursome fell back into their chairs and just looked at each other.

"Are you thinking what I'm thinking?" Marion asked as she wiped the tears from her eyes.

Glenda nodded. "Duncan."

"It was his Powerball number," Ralph said.

"Yes, it was," Glenda confirmed. "I would never have picked 32. But I decided to throw in the extra dollar. So you all owe me a quarter!"

"I'll even pay you interest," Tommy promised.

They all laughed, but immediately their expressions turned serious. "We should share this with Duncan," Glenda said. "The poor guy. He wouldn't even treat himself to a burger tonight. And without his number, we wouldn't have won."

"And we wouldn't have won if you hadn't thrown in that extra dollar," Marion said. "How can we all ever thank you?"

Glenda smiled. "We've been in this together for years,

and now we've been blessed. Let's start our own Festival of Joy. I can't wait to hear Duncan's reaction." She pulled out her cell phone. Duncan's numbers were in her list of contacts. She tried his home phone and his cell, but he didn't pick up either one. She left a message for him to call immediately, no matter what time it was. "That's strange," she said when she hung up. "He certainly sounded as if he were going straight home. I wonder if he knows yet that our numbers won and thinks he's not part of it."

"He might think that you just played our four dollars and we lost out," Tommy said.

At that moment the bartender came over, uncorked a bottle of champagne, and started to pour it into four glasses. "Time to celebrate. I'm sure none of you are planning to go to work in the morning."

"You bet we're not," Marion said. "This is the new Mrs. Conklin's big chance to run the whole show. Let her try and bake a cake as good as mine. Good luck, honey!"

They clinked glasses as they nodded in rapturous agreement at the thought of the expression on The Skunk's face when she heard of their good fortune.

But Glenda couldn't put the nagging worry about Duncan out of her mind. He had been so upset about not getting a bonus, and now he wasn't answering his phone.

Could anything have happened to him?

# 2

Alvirah and Willy Meehan were leaving the Pierre Hotel in New York City where they'd just attended a fundraising dinner for one of Alvirah's favorite charities. Alvirah had been so busy talking to everyone who stopped by the table to say hello, she barely had a bite of food. Willy, who had ended up eating both their meals, was more than ready to go home. It was nearly eleven o'clock and the cocktail hour had started at six. Even the emcee of the event, by the time he finished reading the raffle numbers, seemed a tad weary as he thanked everyone for coming.

It wasn't a long walk to their apartment, but Willy hailed a cab. The night was cold, and Alvirah was wearing high heels. They were also getting up early to drive to a Christmas festival in New Hampshire with their close friends, the private investigator Regan Reilly, her husband, Jack, head of the NYPD Major Case Squad, and Regan's parents, suspense writer Nora Regan Reilly and her husband, Luke, a funeral director. As Willy started to speak to the driver, Alvirah tugged his arm. He knew exactly what that meant. She was hungry. Always agreeable, instead of saying 211 Central Park South, he gave the address of the all-night diner they favored at times like this. "Leo's, 45th and Broadway."

Alvirah sighed contentedly. "Oh, Willy. I know how tired you are. But I'm starving. I'll just get a bowl of Leo's delicious minestrone and a grilled cheese sandwich, then I'll sleep like a baby."

It was not in Willy's nature to say that Alvirah always slept like a baby, no matter what she had or hadn't eaten before bed. But he certainly knew she'd barely had a chance to swallow a morsel tonight. Sometimes he thought she worked harder now than when she was cleaning houses and he was repairing leaky pipes. A few years ago, when they were in their early sixties, they'd won 40 million dollars in the lottery. These days Alvirah wrote a column for the New York *Globe*, involved herself in numerous charities, was the founder of the Lottery Winners Support Group, but most of all had perfected her nose for sniffing out other people's troubles. That he could have done without.

Because of her work as an amateur detective, Alvirah had been injected with poison, had almost been asphyxiated, and had jumped off a cruise ship to escape gunshots.

It's a miracle she doesn't suffer from Post-Traumatic Stress Disorder, Willy thought, as the cab pulled up to Leo's.

"We'll make this quick, honey," Alvirah promised as Willy paid the fare. "We can sit at the counter."

Inside Leo's they were almost knocked out by the odor of a strong cleaning solution that was being sloshed around the floor by a bored looking worker. A yellow sign warned, "Caution. Wet Floor."

"Oh boy," Alvirah groaned. She turned to Willy as they were about to sit down. "I didn't think they used that kind of eye-stinging junk anymore. There aren't many things in this world that can kill my appetite, but the smell of that stuff is one of them. Let's get out of here."

Willy was thrilled. He couldn't wait to get home. He could just visualize getting under the covers and leaning back into his pillow on their big comfortable bed. At that moment, Leo came out from the kitchen. Willy waved at him. "We're not staying."

"Leo, what kind of insecticide are you using in that bucket?" Alvirah asked.

"It's pretty awful," Leo agreed. "The new supplier talked me into it. It's supposed to kill every germ known to man."

"I've got news, Leo. It's killing *me*," Alvirah said, as she started toward the exit. But she hadn't taken three steps when she started to slip on the wet tile. In a futile gesture, Willy lunged to steady her. Alvirah managed to break her fall by grabbing a stool, but her upper body snapped forward, and she hit her head on the Formica countertop.

An hour later they were in the emergency room of St. Luke's Hospital, waiting for a plastic surgeon to close up the cut above her left eyebrow.

"Mrs. Meehan, you're one tough lady," a young intern had said admiringly after he read her X-ray. "You don't have a concussion, and your blood pressure is fine. The plastic surgeon will be here any minute, and you'll be good as new."

"I want his references," Alvirah said, raising her good eyebrow. "Just tonight I saw enough blank faces to know there's at least one lousy plastic surgeon on the loose in this city."

"Don't worry. Dr. Freize is the best."

Dr. Freize might have been the best, but his words that were meant to be caring, rubbed Alvirah the wrong way. As he finished stitching her wound, he said softly, "Now I want you to go home and rest very quietly over the weekend."

Alvirah's eyes flew open. "We're going to New Hampshire in the morning for a Festival of Joy. I don't want to miss it."

"I'm sure you don't," Dr. Freize agreed. "But you must consider your age."

Alvirah bristled.

"I keep reminding Alvirah we're not spring chickens," Willy tried to joke.

"You're not," the doctor confirmed. "You must take my advice. Stay home."

# 3

Agitated and heartsick, Duncan drove home to his tiny rented house on Huckleberry Lane. Twenty minutes from Conklin's Market, his abode was located at the far end of a heavily wooded dead-end street.

"No bonus!" he kept exclaiming as he gripped the wheel of his "previously owned" eleven-year-old SUV. "No bonus! How am I going to pay for Flower's ring?" He'd spotted the ring in the window of Pettie's Fine Jewelry last June, and even though he and Flower had just met once, after having found each other online, he already knew she was the one. The setting of the ring was shaped like a flower with a little diamond in the center and semiprecious stones in the surrounding petals. Mr. Pettie had begrudgingly agreed to accept a modest down payment and set it aside until Christmas.

Now what was he going to do? He could put the ring on his credit card, but everyone knew that if you didn't pay the balance in full at the end of the month, you were socked with sky-high interest charges that just kept on accumulating.

Last month a pair of investment experts had come to town to conduct a weekly seminar on financial planning that would wrap up before Christmas. Duncan, already planning for his future with Flower, had eagerly signed up for the course. After last Wednesday night's class, the experts, Edmund and Woodrow Winthrop, cousins in their early fifties, had called him aside. "We have been given the opportunity to buy shares in an oil drilling company that promises to return ten times our investment within the year. It's a home run," Edmund whispered.

"A grand slam!" Woodrow corrected.

"There is room for only one more person to invest $5,000. From the financial statement you filled out for us, we see that you have $5,000 in your savings account. Having it sit in the bank like that, Duncan, you're losing money. We like you. You're a hard working, conscientious young man, and you deserve an incredible opportunity like this . . ."

"I . . . I . . . I . . . don't know," Duncan stammered.

"Your concern is understandable," Edmund said soothingly. "We're each putting in a hundred thousand. That's as much as the company officers will let us invest."

"A hundred thousand each!" Duncan had been awed.

"I wish they'd let us put in more," Edmund said. "But that's the law. Duncan, if you want to get in on this, the offer closes tomorrow at noon . . ."

The next morning Duncan was at the bank when it opened, switched all the money from his savings to his checking account, then drove to the house where the Winthrops were living and conducting the seminar. With mixed emotions of anticipation and anxiety, he handed them the check. It was the first time Duncan had been late for work in years.

Now he had no bonus, no savings, and Flower's ring was still sitting in the safe at Pettie's. She was flying in from California late next week, and he planned to propose to her on Christmas Eve.

As he got closer to home, the light snowfall was becoming thicker, but Duncan barely noticed. When he pulled into his driveway and turned off the engine, it made a sputtering noise that was new to the car's various creaks and groans. Another worry, Duncan thought, as he got out, slammed the door behind him, and made a dash up the slippery path.

Inside the chilly house, which Duncan now kept at a thrifty 64 degrees, he shrugged off his coat and threw it on the couch. The first thing he spotted were all the notes he had taken at the financial planning course. They were on the dining room table where he pored over them after every session. Edmund and Woodrow's lecture last night had been about how people waste their hard-earned money. He recalled every word.

"Do you know how much money you spend a year on

those cups of coffee you buy every day? Make a Thermos of coffee and bring it to work or keep it in your car," Edmund had counseled, his thin face set in a worried frown. He'd taken off his glasses and, twirling them for emphasis, intoned, "Every time you walk out of your house without a Thermos, you're cheating yourself of money that will add to the comfort of your retirement."

Woodrow, his beefy face always wreathed in smiles, interrupted his cousin. "Excuse me, Eddie," he said, "but I have a question for our guests." He pointed at the seventeen Branscombe townspeople attending the seminar. "How many of you rinse out those plastic bags in the refrigerator and reuse them?"

No one had raised a hand.

"Just what I thought!" he boomed, then spotted one hand timidly ascending into the air. "Mrs. Potters, I'm so proud of you." He got up from his chair, hurried over, and reached for the elderly former school teacher's hand. She beamed as he raised it to his lips.

"What I was going to say," she said sweetly, "is that I did start saving plastic bags and reusing them, but I found it didn't always work out that well. I put my late husband's leftover birthday cake, the last birthday cake he ever had on earth, in a bag that had been used for Roquefort cheese, and let me tell you, it was the first time I ever heard him use a swear word." She smiled up at Woodrow, who had dropped her hand.

"Thank you for sharing that with us, Mrs. Potters," he said. "But the occasional little glitch on our path to financial wisdom is to be expected."

Mrs. Potters nodded briefly. "I suppose."

Woodrow hurried back to the front of the room. "Folks, we'll wind up with some final useful hints that you can take home, mull over, and hopefully act on. Buy washable clothes! Dry cleaning is expensive. And for goodness sake, and most important, don't waste your money on lottery tickets. You may just as well take a match to your money and burn it. Good night, everyone. We'll see you next week. Drive safely. Remember, walk whenever possible. It's good exercise and it saves gas."

Duncan, because of their kindness in letting him in on their investment, and feeling something akin to being the teacher's pet, had gone up to them after class. "Hey, guys, I love your advice, but I can't agree with you about the lottery. A group of us at work buy tickets together. We all throw in a dollar twice a week and like the ad on the commercial says, 'Hey, you never know!' "

Edmund and Woodrow had shaken their heads with amused disdain. "Duncan, that's 104 dollars a year that you could invest in something that promises a real return."

But Duncan was happy and in love and looking forward to seeing his Flower. "I have to play just one more time," he said. "I just feel lucky. We play the same numbers always but take turns on selecting the Powerball on our last ticket. Tomorrow is my day to choose. My birthday is next week and I'm turning thirty-two, so that's what I'm going to play."

"32 huh?" Woodrow said with a grin.

"32!" Duncan crowed. He recited the rest of the numbers slowly, as if he were chanting, "5, 15, 23, 44, and 52. We've been playing them for years."

"5, 15, 23, 44 and 52," Edmund repeated slowly. "I suppose they stand for birthdays and anniversaries and street addresses."

"Or the day someone's tooth fell out," Woodrow laughed heartily.

"No, not that," Duncan laughed with him. "But the numbers 5, 15, 23, 44, and 52 do mean something to each of us."

"So what," Woodrow said. "We still think you're wasting your money. I hope when we see you next time, you'll be able to tell us that you resisted temptation." He slapped Duncan on the back.

Now, standing alone in his little house, Duncan was anxious to talk to Flower but decided he should wait until he had calmed down. She was so sweet and kind, and so sensitive to his feelings that she would know right away by the tone of his voice that he was upset about something. And what could he tell her? That he didn't get the bonus he expected, had invested all his savings, and now didn't have the money to pay for her engagement ring?

Disgusted with himself, he threw down his cell phone, went into the kitchen, opened the refrigerator, and pulled out a bottle of beer. He took it into the living room, plopped down on his La-Z-Boy, leaned back, and sighed as the footrest rose and snapped in place. From here he had a perfect view of the picture of Flower he had taken on their first date at a restaurant on the wharf in San Francisco. When he walked in, she had been sitting with her hands folded on the table, looking out at the water. She heard him approach the table, turned, and smiled, a small sweet smile that lit up her face and Duncan's heart.

They had started talking and never seemed to stop. With so much in common, including hippy parents, they had traded stories of falling asleep at protests, eating organic food, and changing schools numerous times when they were growing up. Flower had been named Flower because her parents worked for a landscaper. "It could be worse," Flower had laughed. "My father wanted to name me Shrub."

"Mom and Dad named me Duncan because they met at Dunkin' Donuts, waiting in line for takeout coffee," he told her. It was unbelievable to him that after such a nomadic childhood his parents were now living in an over-55 community in Florida, and enjoying bingo nights.

Duncan and Flower had talked about their need for roots. He was delighted when he heard that several times a year she took a bus trip to Lake Tahoe from her apartment in San Francisco. She, like him, loved snow. She loved her job at a day care center for pre-school children, even though it didn't pay very well. But most important, now she loves me, he thought, as he flipped on the television and leaned back further.

I have to count my blessings. Money isn't everything. We have our health. We're better off than 99.9 percent of the people in the world. So cheer up, he scolded himself, it's only money. Maybe Mr. Pettie will let me have the ring now, and I'll arrange to pay it off in monthly installments. He has to know I'm good for it.

Duncan drank his beer as he watched the last thirty minutes of a crime program about a woman con artist who had married four men and cleaned them out of every cent they had. They must have been some dopes he thought as his eyes began to close.

An hour later, the sound of a strident voice filled with phony excitement jolted him awake. When Duncan realized what the announcer was saying, that there were two winners who bought lottery tickets ten miles apart in New Hampshire, he bolted forward, his chair moving with him. He wanted to cover his ears when the announcer started to read the winning numbers, but he didn't.

By the time the third number was read, his heart was pounding. *Our* numbers! he thought frantically. The next two were also their numbers. It can't be, he thought. But when the announcer said, with a big smile, that the Powerball number was 32, Duncan jumped up like a shot.

"I didn't play!" he screamed. "I didn't play! We could have won!" He froze. Could Glenda have used his Powerball number anyway? If she did, and they have one of the winning tickets, I'm not in on it, thanks to those Winthrop idiots!

The uneasy feeling that he'd been trying to ignore about investing his savings in an oil well exploded inside him. Suddenly the whole idea seemed ridiculous.

I want my money back right now!

He grabbed his coat and ran out the door. They've ruined my life, he thought wildly as he got into his car, pumped the pedal, and turned the key in the ignition.

He was rewarded for his efforts by dead silence.

"Come on!" he cried impatiently, as he kept turning the key. He didn't want to even think about the fact that if he had played the lottery he could go out and buy any car he wanted. Even a Rolls-Royce!

"Come *on!*" he cried again, angry tears glistening in his eyes. Finally he pounded the steering wheel and got out.

Half-crazed, he began to run down the darkened street, ignoring the snow that pelted his face and hair. With the speed of an arrow shot from a bow, he raced toward the house the financial wizards had rented for their one-month stay in Branscombe.

Twenty minutes later, huffing and puffing, he was running up the Winthrops' driveway, heading for the side door, which was the entrance for the classes. It opened onto the rec room where the chairs and blackboard were set up. As he was about to ring the bell, he heard shouts from within the house. What's going on? he wondered. It sounds like something's wrong.

With an instinctive gesture, he turned the handle of the door. It was unlocked. He pushed it open and could hear the Winthrops' loud, almost hysterically pitched voices, coming from the kitchen. The kitchen, living, and dining rooms were a half level above the makeshift classroom. The door at the top of the staircase to the kitchen was closed. Duncan moved swiftly across the tired brown carpet, stopped at the bottom of the staircase, and listened. What he heard next confirmed his worst fears.

"Hey, Edmund, do you think any of the dopes in this town would buy the Brooklyn Bridge if we tried to sell it to them?"

Edmund laughed heartily. "I know who'd buy it."

"Duncan Donuts!"

They both guffawed. One of them was obviously pounding a table.

"Duncan's as dumb as the guy in Arizona who invested in windmills in Alaska last year. If he only knew . . ."

"Can you just see the look on his face if he ever found out that we used his lottery numbers and have a winning ticket?"

"I want a front row seat for that."

They were guffawing again.

"Do you think there's any chance he didn't follow our

sage advice and went in on the ticket anyhow with his Powerball number?"

"Nah. I think we bowled him over too well with our wisdom. But the other winning ticket *was* sold in this town. Can you imagine if his coworkers won with his Powerball number? Wouldn't that be a scream?"

Duncan's head felt as though it would burst open.

This is a living nightmare, he thought. They're phonies, they're crooks—they stole my money *and* they stole my lottery numbers. After they told me not to play! Tears that he'd held back on his run through the streets flowed down his frozen cheeks. I know what I'll do, he thought. I'll call the FBI! I'll make sure those two creeps spend the rest of their lives in orange jumpsuits. Jumpsuits you don't have to dry clean, he thought bitterly.

Just then, he heard movement in his direction and thought he saw the kitchen doorknob start to turn. Panicked, he knew he didn't have time to get out of the house without being seen. He darted to the left, opened the door that led to the basement, and disappeared behind it. As he pulled the door closed, his wet shoe slipped on the top step, and he tumbled down the stairs.

He landed hard on the cement floor. The pain that shot through his right leg caused beads of sweat to form on his forehead. Did they hear me? he wondered fearfully. If they ever thought that I overheard what they were saying, my goose is cooked. I'd never see my little Flower again.

"Edmund, what was that noise?"

"Oh no," Duncan whispered.

"Must be the old furnace. This place is the pits. Give me another beer."

"Should we check and make sure?"

"Why bother?"

Thank you, God, Duncan thought as the boisterous activities overhead continued. Through the heating grates he could clearly hear them ridiculing the stupidity of the various suckers they had cheated and their hilarity about having legitimately won the mega-mega millions with "Duncan Donut's" numbers.

They're dangerous, he thought. Sheer panic made his heart race. He tried to move his body, but the pain in his leg made him feel dizzy.

How am I ever going to make it out of here? he wondered as he lay there in the dark, dank basement. An incongruous thought raced through his head. I wish I had taken Glenda up on her suggestion to make myself a peanut butter sandwich.

# 4

None of the winners wanted to be out of the immediate vicinity of the lottery ticket. Not that they didn't love and trust each other, but they'd done the arithmetic. They knew enough about lottery jackpots to know what they could expect from a 180 million dollar share of the pot. They agreed to take the lump sum payment, which would probably be about 88 million. After taxes, it would leave them with, more or less, 60 million. Divided by five, they'd walk away from The Skunk with twelve million dollars each in their pockets.

"Let's have our picture taken when we accept the big check and send it to her!" Marion crowed.

They all decided to spend the night at Ralph's house. He had a big family room with a couple of lounging couches and some overstuffed chairs. Not that any of them expected to get much sleep. But at least they could put their feet up. As they sipped champagne, they called their families.

Ralph's wife, Judy, screeched at the news and was thrilled to host the sleepover.

"I'll make a pot of coffee," she cried. "I can't believe I babysat those brats all night for a lousy thirty bucks! TWELVE MILLION DOLLARS! Ralph, we're finally out of the hole!"

Ralph, a heavyset redhead, who could look a little scary when he had a big carving knife in his hand, started to cry. "We'll call the girls together, honey. I can't wait to hear their reactions."

"I love you, Ralph!" Judy was crying, too.

Tommy called his parents, who were overwhelmed, then as usual his mother managed to worry about something. "Tommy don't get yourself too excited," she cautioned. "You might make yourself sick. Maybe you should come home now."

"Mom, I'm fine! I'm more than fine. I'll call Gina and tell her to get first-class airline tickets for her and Don and the kids to fly in next week. We haven't had Christmas together in a couple of years."

"Oh, Tommy, that would be so wonderful!"

Marion phoned her son in California. "Tell T. J. that his granny is going to give him a wedding present that will knock his socks off! Come to think of it, he'd better get himself a prenuptial agreement!"

Glenda reached her widowed father in Florida. "Dad, I have something I want you to do tomorrow morning," she said exuberantly.

"What's that, honey?" her father asked in a sleepy voice, never reprimanding her for calling so late. How she could have married a creep like Harvey when her father was such a decent human being would take years of therapy to figure out.

"Dad, go out and buy yourself a powerboat like your friend Walter has. No, buy an even bigger one!" She started laughing.

"Glenda, you sound a little tipsy, dear. I hope you're not depressed about that jerk Harvey. . . ."

"I'm not depressed at all, Dad. And I'm not tipsy . . ." It took Glenda a solid three minutes to convince her father that the unbelievable had happened.

As they were leaving the tavern, several of the patrons asked them to pose for pictures.

"We're famous," Marion sighed. "I can't believe we're famous. I wish I'd worn my new pink blouse. The saleslady said the ruffles around the collar were very flattering."

Glenda, who had seen the pink blouse, didn't necessarily agree. I'll go shopping with Marion and help her find an outfit for her grandson's wedding. I have to do some shopping, too, she thought, as she remembered the remark Harvey had made to her outside the courtroom.

"I really wish you the best, Glenda," he'd said. "And I hope you meet someone who loves you just the way you are," he'd added with a snicker.

She knew what he was saying. She needed to lose some

weight and fix herself up but after years of living with his constant little digs she'd given up even trying to look good. That was about to change. And won't Harvey be sorry to miss all the trips I'll be taking, Glenda thought gleefully. I'll start with a makeover at a spa, just like that lottery winner Alvirah Meehan who is supposed to come to the Festival this weekend with her friend Nora Regan Reilly. If Alvirah does show up, I'd love to get the chance to talk to her.

Ralph's house was fifteen minutes away. Charley, a sixtyish chauffeur who had the only stretch limo in town, had just walked into the tavern after driving an accounting firm's employees home from their company Christmas party. During the month of December he was hired for a lot of those jobs, advertising himself as "Your Designated Driver." Now he insisted on escorting the brand new millionaires to Ralph's in grand style.

"Leave your cars in the lot here. I'd be honored to give this group their first ride together in a stretch limo." Then he added ruefully, "I knew I should have taken a job at Conklin's years ago. I might be sharing this with you. Oh well."

Climbing into the limo, in deference to the weather they started to sing: "Dashing through the snow . . ." When they reached Ralph's driveway, the front door of his house flew open. Judy half-ran, half-skidded down the path, pulled open the back door of the limo, and dove in, throwing her arms around Ralph. "We're rich!" she screamed. "I never thought I'd utter those two words in this lifetime, honey, but we're rich! A reporter from that network covering the Festival has called three times. He heard from somebody at the tavern about the winning ticket. BUZ wants an interview with all of you."

"Do you think we should be like Paris Hilton and hire bodyguards?" Marion asked in a worried tone. "After all, we have a little piece of paper that's worth millions."

"I've got it right here, Marion," Glenda said reassuringly, patting her purse."

Inside the modest but warmly decorated home, they gathered at the dining room table, which Judy had set with her good china cups and dessert plates. A Christmas tree was twinkling in the living room. It was obvious that Judy loved to decorate for the holidays. There wasn't a square inch of space—on the walls or table tops—that didn't contain a Christmasy knickknack. Lighted Christmas candles glowed on the sideboard and table.

Judy began to pour the coffee, but her hands were trembling. It was all she could do to avoid slopping it into the saucers. As though thinking aloud, she said, "I'm fifty years old and I've hardly ever been out of New Hampshire. Ralph and I have been together since high school." She looked at her husband. "After we take that cruise, I want to go to London and Paris and Rome." Then she glanced down at her well-worn sweater and jeans. "And I want new clothes." She shook her head. "I still can't believe this is real. Can I see the ticket?"

Glenda carefully took the ticket out of her wallet and handed it to her.

"Don't get too close to any of the candles!" Marion warned.

Over coffee and cupcakes they talked about how it would feel when they walked into the convenience store as it opened at seven and had their ticket confirmed. And how they'd feel when they didn't report to work.

Marion showed Judy the framed photo that had been their Christmas bonus.

"That's disgraceful," Judy said as she read the inscription. "The Skunk deserves what she gets and so does he. Old Man Conklin certainly knows that you guys depend, or should I say depended, on that bonus. They're going to have some job catering the Festival of Joy without you."

"I would have gone in to help out if it weren't for that so-called Christmas gift," Glenda said.

The phone rang. This time it was the producer from BUZ. They arranged to meet him and his crew at the convenience store at seven.

As Ralph and Judy called their daughters, Glenda phoned Duncan again. But he didn't answer. "I just hope he decided to turn off his phone and go to sleep," she said, trying to sound cheerful.

"I'm sure he's fine," Tommy reassured her. "When Charley picks us up in the morning we can swing by Duncan's house and collect him. He's bound to be up, getting ready for work. We'll tell him that we voted him in on the winning ticket." Tommy whooped, "I can't wait to see the look on his face!"

# 5

## Friday, December 12th

It was nearly 2 A.M. when Willy and the somewhat battered Alvirah finally arrived home to 211 Central Park South. As they climbed into bed, Willy turned off the alarm clock that had been set for an early start to New Hampshire.

"I was really looking forward to the Festival," Alvirah sighed. "It sounded like so much fun." Regretfully she glanced at their already packed bags. "We've all been so busy that we haven't seen that much of the Reillys, and I miss them."

"We'll go next year," Willy promised. "While you were changing, I sent an e-mail to Regan and Jack and explained what happened. I said you were fine, but we wouldn't be able to join them this weekend and we'd call them later." Then as he turned off the light, he said, "Be sure to wake me up if you don't feel well. That was some whack you got."

When he received no response, he realized Alvirah was already asleep. What a surprise, he thought as he cuddled up to her.

Seven hours later, when Alvirah opened her eyes, she felt completely refreshed. Instinctively she raised her hand and applied tentative pressure to the bandage on her forehead. It's sore but no big deal, she thought. Willy insisted on serving her breakfast in bed. Fifteen minutes later, propped up on three pillows, she quickly dispatched the scrambled eggs he had carefully prepared.

Swallowing her final bite of toast, Alvirah daintily dabbed her mouth with an apricot-colored cloth napkin that had been bought to coordinate with the breakfast tray. "Willy I really feel fine," she said. "Let's go to the Festival."

"Alvirah, you heard what the doctor said. We'll make it next year. Just relax." He picked up the tray. "Let me get you another cup of tea."

"Why not?" Alvirah grumbled. "I've certainly got nothing else to do." She reached for the remote control and flicked on the television. "Let's see what's going on in the rest of the world." She pressed the number of the BUZ network. Immediately the face of Cliff Bailey, the handsome anchorman who had interviewed her about the pitfalls of being a lottery winner, filled the screen. Alvirah remembered telling him there shouldn't be any pitfalls but unfortunately some people went crazy when they got their hands on so much cash.

"And now an unbelievable story," Bailey said breathlessly, "coming out of the town of Branscombe, New Hampshire, where a group of four coworkers at the local market won half the 360 million dollar mega-mega lottery last night."

"Alvirah, would you like another piece of toast?" Willy called from the kitchen.

"Shhhhh" Alvirah ordered as she turned up the volume and shouted, "Willy, get in here!"

Not knowing what to expect, Willy hurried into the bedroom.

". . . the other winning ticket was bought in Red Oak, a town ten miles away from Branscombe. In the history of the lottery, lightning has never struck twice in towns so close to each other. The owner of the second winning ticket has not yet come forward. In Branscombe, however, there is both concern and speculation. A fifth coworker, Duncan Graham, who had been playing the group lottery for years, decided only yesterday to no longer participate. Even so, his friends intend to share the pot with him as it was his choice of the Powerball number that clinched the prize. But he has disappeared without a trace. Duncan hasn't been seen since he left the market last night. Some skeptics think he might have played the numbers on his own, now holds the other winning ticket, and is embarrassed to face his coworkers who immediately after winning left him a message promising to cut him in. Here's a shot of the four coworkers as they validated their lottery ticket this morning."

Alvirah quickly studied the expressions on the faces of the two men and two women. Their smiles seemed somewhat forced. They looked bewildered rather than exuberant. "I can't believe we're not there yet," Alvirah cried as she threw back the covers. Willy took one look at her. He knew there was no use arguing. "I'll do the dishes and make the bed while you take a shower."

"Call the garage and tell them to get the car out pronto. At least we didn't unpack our suitcases. I could wring that doctor's neck for ordering me to stay home. He's never met me before in his life—what does he know about my constitution? In the old days, if I'd gotten three stitches over my eye, I wouldn't have dreamed of calling Mrs. O'Keefe and telling her I couldn't show up to clean her messy house. I would have been out of a job. Willy, get Regan on the phone and tell her we're on the way."

The bathroom door snapped shut behind Alvirah.

"I knew we'd end up at that Festival," Willy muttered as he began to make the bed.

# 6

Regan and Jack Reilly left their Tribeca loft at 7 A.M. in the large SUV they had rented for the weekend. The plan had been to pick up Regan's parents and Alvirah and Willy Meehan from their neighboring apartments on Central Park South, then they'd all ride together to New Hampshire. The disappointing e-mail from Willy that he and Alvirah would not be able to join them had made the larger vehicle not only unnecessary, but also a continuing reminder of Alvirah and Willy's absence.

Regan's mother, Nora Regan Reilly, chic even at this early hour, glanced wistfully up at Alvirah's building as she got into the car. A casual bystander would have known immediately that Regan was bone of her bone and flesh of her flesh. They shared fair skin, startling blue eyes, and classic features. Where they differed was in hair color and height. Nora was a petite blonde, while Regan had inherited raven black hair from her father's side of the family, and at 5'7" also carried the tall genes of the Reillys. Her father, Luke, was a lanky, silver-haired 6'5".

"I hope Alvirah is going to be all right," Nora worried as she settled in the car.

Luke tossed their suitcases in the back and climbed in beside her. "My bet's on Alvirah," he said. "I feel sorry for the counter."

"That was exactly my thought, but I was afraid Regan would get mad if I said it," Jack agreed. His hazel eyes twinkled as he glanced back over his shoulder at Luke. Jack Reilly had a very special affection for his father-in-law. It was because Luke had been kidnapped by the disgruntled relative of a man he had buried from one of his funeral homes that Jack had first met Regan. As head of the NYPD Major Case Squad, Jack had been called in. Sandy-haired and handsome, with a commanding presence, at thirty-four years old Jack was one of the rising stars of New York's finest. A Boston College graduate, he had elected not to go into the family investment firm, but instead chose the career path of his paternal grandfather. During Regan and Jack's courtship, he became known as Jack "no relation" Reilly.

Two hours later, after fighting the usual Friday morning traffic, the Reillys were well into the state of Connecticut when Jack's cell phone rang. He fished it from his pocket, glanced at the caller ID, and handed it to Regan. "It's Mayor Steve," he said. "Tell him I'm driving. You know me, I'm a law-abiding citizen."

"That's why I married you," Regan said with a smile as she took the phone. "Hello, Steve . . ." she began, then listened as a torrent of information filled her ear. "You're kidding!" she finally managed to interject. "We've been listening to music and traffic reports. I guess we should have turned on the news."

Bursting with curiosity, Nora bolted forward, her body straining the seat belt. Beside her, Luke leaned back, "Tell me if they need my services," he drawled.

Regan tried to ignore the fact that Nora was making gestures for her to hold out the phone. "Yes, Steve, we should definitely be at the Inn by twelve for the press conference."

"Press conference!" Nora exclaimed.

"At ease, sweetie," Luke said mildly, raising his eyebrows as he caught Jack's amused glance in the rear view mirror.

"Okay, Steve, try not to worry too much. The Festival will be a success, I'm sure. We'll see you at the Inn." Regan snapped the cell phone closed. She leaned back. "I'm so tired, I think I'll just close my eyes for a few minutes."

Nora was appalled. "Regan!"

Jack poked his bride in the ribs. "Spit it out."

"Welllllll, if you insist," Regan began. "As you know the Festival of Joy starts this afternoon. Last night a group of employees from the local market that will be catering the Festival won half the mega-mega 360 million dollar lottery."

"There go the bologna sandwiches," Luke muttered.

"And the potato salad," Jack added.

"Will you two please be quiet so Regan can talk?" Nora asked, trying not to laugh. "Regan, go on."

"In a nutshell, there were five workers who always went in on the lottery. This time one of them, at the last minute, decided not to play."

"Poor devil," Luke sighed.

"The others intended to share the lottery with him because he had picked the Powerball number. But he hasn't been seen since he left work last night. They can tell he went home—his car is still in the driveway—but he's not there and doesn't answer his cell phone. They're afraid something happened to him."

"What a shame," Nora said. "Do they think that if he realized he had lost out on the lottery . . ." She stopped not wanting to voice the possibility that was occurring to all of them.

"It gets more complicated," Regan continued. "Another winning ticket was sold a couple of towns away. Some people suspect that after refusing to throw in his dollar with the others, this guy Duncan bought his own ticket and is embarrassed to admit it."

"Oh, well, that's a different story," Luke said. "I started to feel sorry for him, but I bet you anything he's recovering from his shame on a tropical beach with a piña colada in one hand and the winning ticket in the other."

"I guess that would be the best outcome," Nora said, her mystery writer's mind considering the possibilities.

"Apparently the whole town is talking about the lottery instead of the Festival, and the television producer cancelled Steve and Muffy's interview this morning. He's too busy following the lottery story."

"No interview for Muffy?" Luke exclaimed. "Jack, you'd better step on it."

"Dad, don't be mean," Regan protested. "Steve sounds very upset."

"I think he hoped this Festival would help raise his profile in New Hampshire," Jack explained.

"Sounds like it's working," Luke drawled.

"From what I can tell," Jack observed, "Steve wants to go places in politics, and Muffy sees herself as the next Jackie Kennedy. In college Steve was always organizing everything. We called him Mayor Steve back then."

Regan gasped. "I just had a thought. Can you imagine Alvirah's reaction when she finds out what she's missing?" At that moment her cell phone rang.

"No need to check your caller ID, Regan," Luke said. "Dollars to donuts, Alvirah just got wind of what's happening in Branscombe."

"No doubt," Jack agreed. "And we'll be seeing her before the sun goes down."

# 7

**W**here am I? Duncan asked himself as he opened his eyes. What happened? Then it all came back to him: He had fallen down the stairs and was lying on the cold cement floor in the basement of the house those idiot crooks were inhabiting. Faint light was coming through the gritty windows, and he could see that it was snowing lightly. He remembered that he had been awake for hours, hungry and in pain, forced to listen to the Winthrops celebrating their good fortune. When they finally went to bed, he must have dozed off. It was the smell of coffee wafting through the grates that woke him. The same grates that had allowed the bragging voices of the cheats to insult his ears.

Every bone in Duncan's body ached, but it was his right leg that was really sore. He wondered if he had broken it. Last night, after the shock of the fall, it had hurt too much to move it.

"Coffee, Eddie?" he heard from above.

Here we go, Duncan thought. Plato and Aristotle are ready to take on the day. I've got to get out of here. But how?

"I could use some," Edmund answered. "And a couple of aspirin. How many beers did we have last night?"

"Who knows? Who cares? I don't even know what time we went to bed."

"With all our money we should be in a palace, having a butler serve us coffee instead of drinking from chipped mugs in this crummy dump."

"It won't be long," Woodrow crowed. "Can you imagine if Grandpa saw us now? He always said neither one of us would amount to anything."

Grandpa was right, Duncan thought as he turned on his side, sat up, and brushed his hair back from his forehead. I want some of that coffee. He licked his lips. His mouth was so dry. What I'd really love is a tall glass of fresh orange juice. And bacon and eggs and bagels. But I can't think about food now. If those guys ever decide to come down here, I'm dead.

Woodrow wouldn't shut up. "I wish we could just blow this town today. But if we skip the final class next week, people who paid for our great advice will start comparing notes. Once they realize almost all of them were in on the oil well investment, we'll have the cops on our tail."

Duncan felt as if he'd been slapped in the face. He knew it was stupid, but he felt betrayed yet again. I never was meant to be the teacher's pet, he thought forlornly. I've been such a fool.

"We can't leave for good, but why don't we drive down to Boston for the day and celebrate? I might even buy my ex-wife a present. That would really be the Christmas spirit," Edmund said, laughing heartily.

"I'm not buying anything for mine. I still can't believe she never once visited me in the clink," Woodrow said, not sounding the least bit upset.

"She did the first time we were in," Edmund reminded his cousin.

"Yes, but all she did was complain. Some visit."

I may be forced to kill myself, Duncan thought.

"Who cares about them?" Edmund said. "With the kind of money we'll have falling out of our pockets, we'll have no trouble meeting girls. Speaking of our future millions, if we go to Boston today, what should we do with the ticket? Do you think it's safe to carry it?"

"With all those pickpockets out during the holiday season? No way. We'd better leave the ticket here," Woodrow said emphatically.

"Where? What if the house burns down while we're gone?"

"We'll leave it in the freezer."

Duncan's eyes widened, and his heart began to race. He held his breath as he waited for Edmund's response. Come on Edmund, he thought. Go for the freezer!

"The freezer?" Edmund asked doubtfully. "I don't know . . . maybe we better just take the ticket with us."

"No," Duncan moaned. He thought of the audiences at

game shows who yelled advice to contestants. "No, Eddie, no! Go for the freezer!" Duncan wanted to yell.

"It's the safest place," Woodrow insisted. "We'll put it in a plastic bag. I've heard stories of people losing their lottery tickets because they were carrying them around. Can you imagine how we'd feel if that happened?"

"It's too awful to think about," Edmund said with a shudder. "There'd be no living with you."

"Me? Look who's talking!"

They both laughed.

"Okay, we'll leave it in the freezer," Edmund finally agreed. "What a joke that we broke parole again by spending a buck on a lottery ticket. Next week when we finish up here, we'll figure where to cash it in and who can front for us. We have a year to decide."

"A year?" Woodrow yelled. "Are you nuts? I'm not waiting a year. You call yourself a financial expert? Every day we wait we're losing interest."

"Of course we're not going to wait a year. We just have to figure it all out . . . Hey, it's almost eleven o'clock. Let's get showered and get out of here. This place gets on my nerves. No wonder they were willing to rent it for a month."

By the time they returned to the kitchen half an hour later, Duncan had come up with a plan, that if successful, would give him infinite pleasure for the rest of his life.

"Woodrow, don't leave it in plain sight," Edmund was saying, his voice clearly annoyed. "Put the bag under that box of frozen peas."

Frozen peas? Duncan thought. My fresh ones taste so much better.

"Okay. There. Are you happy? It's under the peas."

Duncan heard the slam of the front door followed by the sound of their car starting up. They're gone! he thought. All was silent except for the groan of the furnace. I'm alone in a house with a lottery ticket worth 180 million dollars, he thought. Who needs more motivation than that to drag himself off the floor? He reached for the bannister and strained to pull himself up, resting all his weight on his left leg. Gingerly he touched his right foot to the floor and winced. Mind over matter, he told himself. Leaning heavily on the wobbly bannister he hopped slowly up the stairs, opened the door, and continued to hop the few steps to the staircase that led to the kitchen.

The sound of a car passing in front of the house made Duncan hold his breath. But the car didn't stop. That could have been them coming back, he thought. I've got to hurry.

Despite the fact that he was supporting his entire weight on one leg, he made it up the steps and across the small kitchen in record time. No wonder the owner can't sell this place, Duncan thought. Everything here looks as though it's falling apart. Who cares? he asked himself as he reached the aging refrigerator and opened the freezer door. With quivering fingers he grabbed the carton of peas. This brand went out of business ten years ago, he realized with disgust, then feasted his eyes on the plastic bag containing the lottery ticket. Plucking it from the shelf he turned around, hopped over to the wooden kitchen table, and removed the ticket from the bag. He took a split second to verify the winning numbers—his numbers—and then pulled out his wallet. He tucked the ticket inside, then tenderly reached into another compartment for the lottery ticket he and Flower had bought on their first date. Even though she didn't care much about the lottery, they had enjoyed choosing the numbers together.

"We didn't win that day," Duncan said aloud, "but I knew this ticket would come to some good." Holding it to his lips, he kissed it once, twice, three times, then placed it in the plastic bag. A few seconds later he was returning the bag to where the Winthrops had left it, under the carton of expired peas.

At the sound of a car turning into the driveway, adrenaline shot through his body. It was too late to go back to the basement. With the swiftness of Peter Rabbit, he hopped across the kitchen, into the living room, and ducked behind a large, dilapidated chair.

I'm toast, he thought. If they decided against their road trip to Bean Town and don't leave the house, there's no way they won't discover me.

The door was opening. "All right!" Woodrow snapped

impatiently. "You've said it one hundred times. It's not a good idea to leave the lottery ticket behind."

Duncan could hear him opening the freezer door. His heart stopped.

"You see, it's right here!" Woodrow said. "I'm putting it in my wallet. Or you can put it in your wallet. Tell me what you want."

"I'll take it," Edmund said testily.

Once again, they were on their way.

It's a miracle, Duncan thought. They didn't check the numbers. I've got to get out of here, get home, then figure out what to do. I want the Winthrops to be brought to justice, but I can't blow the whistle on them yet. If I do, they'll either disappear or come back and kill me. And if they disappear, I'll be looking over my shoulder for the rest of my life. I could end up in the Witness Protection Program! Flower and I want to spend our lives in Branscombe.

Deciding the cousins weren't coming back immediately, Duncan pushed himself up. As he was passing the closet by the front door, a thought occurred to him. Maybe there was an umbrella or a cane or something he could lean on inside it. As luck would have it, an old broom crashed to the floor when he opened the door. Leaning down, he unscrewed the pole of the broom from its bristly base. This should help a little, he thought.

Back out in the bracing New Hampshire air, with a 180

million dollar lottery ticket in his wallet, Duncan half hopped, half hobbled down the quiet country road. I just hope I can make it home, he thought. But after he had gone three blocks, he could hear a vehicle pulling over behind him. Nervously he turned around.

It was Enoch Hippogriff, a weather-beaten old-timer who regularly shopped at the market. "Duncan?" he called. "What are you doing here? The whole town is looking for you."

Bewildered but relieved, Duncan dragged himself into Enoch's truck. "Why are they looking for me?" he asked. He wondered if Flower had alerted the authorities when he didn't call her before going to bed, as he always did.

"Don't give me that," Enoch said. "You know why."

"I really don't," Duncan said.

Enoch Hippogriff glanced at him sideways. "You don't, do you? I can tell a man's face. You're a sight, hopping around with that stick in your hand. Duncan, your coworkers won the lottery last night."

"They did!" Duncan exclaimed, mixed emotions charging through his head. "I guess they used the Powerball number I chose after all."

"They used it all right. And even though you didn't throw in a buck, they're cutting you in on it. I don't know if I'd be that good-natured."

Duncan blinked back tears. "They did? Wow! I can't believe how wonderful they are. They really care about me. I want to see them. I don't suppose they went to work . . . I wonder where they all are now."

"They're down at the Branscombe Inn. That's the head-quarters for your search party. Wait till they hear they can call it off!"

"Would you take me there now?" Duncan asked, wondering how he could explain his lost evening.

"Sure," Enoch said, then slapped him on the arm. "The ride will cost you a thousand bucks." His laughter at his own joke led to a fit of coughing. "Yup," he finally said. "It'll be a mere grand. I should charge you more than that! Some people think you disappeared because you're holding the other winning lottery ticket! Isn't that crazy? Just look at you!"

Duncan stared straight ahead as Enoch's old truck rumbled down the road.

So this is how it feels to win the lottery, he thought.

# 8

Horace Pettie and his assistant, Luella, were putting the final touches on the window display that they had created to cash in on the Festival of Joy. Business at Pettie's Fine Jewelry had been slow, and it certainly wasn't being helped by all the emphasis the town was now putting on having a simple, homespun Christmas.

"The message of the Festival is all well and good," Horace said. "But a man has to make a living."

"That's right, Mr. Pettie," Luella chimed in. "It was brilliant of you to create a charm commemorating this weekend. Trust me, it's going to sell like hot cakes," she assured him.

"I think it's really pretty if I say so myself," Pettie admitted, holding up one of the charms. The design was a gold holly wreath with the words "Branscombe's Festival of Joy" engraved around the border. He hadn't wanted to put either a date or the word "First" on the charms in case they didn't sell out. If there happened to be another Festival next year, he could dust off the leftovers.

A small, balding man of sixty-eight, Horace Pettie was another lifetime resident of Branscombe and the sole jeweler in town, as his father had been before him. Luella Cobb, a solid blond woman in her mid-fifties, had been working for him for twenty years, ever since her youngest child started high school. It was the only job she had ever wanted. Ever since Luella had been given a box of play jewelry when she was four years old, she had never been without a bauble or two attached to her body. Her enthusiasm for jewelry made her a splendid saleswoman for Horace Pettie. "Jewelry does not have to be terribly expensive, just tasteful," she would whisper to prospective clients. Then, as surely as night follows day, she'd pull out a more expensive item, breathlessly declaring it "stunning," "gorgeous," and finally exulting, "It's so you!"

Horace laid the last of the little gold holly wreaths on a tiny sled in the window, then he and Luella stepped out onto the sidewalk to view the display. The scene was that of a winter wonderland with Festival charms dangling from red ribbons.

Pettie sighed. "We did a lot of work on this. I hope it brings people into the store."

Luella put her hands on her ample hips. A thoughtful expression crossed her heavily made-up face. It was cold, but they were used to standing outside studying their various displays, so neither one noticed. "Mr. Pettie, I have an idea," Luella said slowly, excitement building in her voice. "I know what we can add to our wonderland that will attract attention."

"What's that, Luella?" Pettie asked, like a mouse snapping at a piece of cheese.

She tapped the window with her manicured finger. "Duncan's ring! Let's place it on the middle of the sled."

"I can't sell Duncan's ring!" Horace protested.

"Not sell it!" Luella said impatiently. "We'll make a sign saying, DUNCAN, COME HOME SOON. WE MISS YOU. YOUR RING IS WAITING."

Horace Pettie's eyes widened. "Duncan is the talk of the town. But don't you think it might seem a little insensitive?"

"Not in the least!" Luella declared. "It's a human interest story. Besides, sensitivity doesn't pay the bills." She turned and went back in the store.

Horace trailed after her, always amazed at Luella's creativity in drumming up business.

"You get the ring out of the safe," Luella ordered.

Horace hesitated.

"Mr. Pettie, don't worry about it. My bet is that Duncan is fine and has that other winning ticket, in which case he'll never come back for the ring."

Horace's ears reddened. "After I held it for him all these months!"

"Exactly!" Luella said. She waved her hand. "If that happens you'll end up selling the ring for twice the price. I'd buy it myself, but I think my husband would kill me."

Horace hurried to the back of the store.

"I'll make up the sign, then get on the phone," Luella called after him. "After I tell Tishie Thornton how bad we feel about poor Duncan, there won't be a living soul within a hundred miles who won't know about that ring in our window. With any luck, a news crew will be here before lunch."

# 9

This is probably the most impulsive thing I've done in my life, Flower thought as she stared out of the window of the bus she had boarded in Concord, New Hampshire. She had been counting the days until she flew in to spend Christmas with Duncan. They had both wished she could be there for the Festival of Joy, even though Duncan would be working, but they knew it didn't make sense. She'd be in for the holidays a week later, and the flights were so expensive. But then the other day, out of the blue, Mrs. Kane had quietly presented her with a check for two thousand dollars.

"Jimmy loves coming to day care, thanks to you," she had whispered to Flower about her three-year-old. "He's always been so terribly shy. You've brought him out of his shell. Please accept this gift, and treat yourself to something very special."

It didn't take Flower long to figure out what that something special would be—a chance to surprise Duncan by showing up in Branscombe for the Festival of Joy. She hoped she'd be allowed to lend a hand with the events Conklin's was catering, so that she could be near Duncan all weekend and get to know the coworkers he always talked about. For the past few months, he'd been hinting he'd bought her something special for Christmas. She hoped against hope that it was an engagement ring.

Flower had been able to get Friday off from work. Before she left for the airport Thursday evening, she had called Duncan, but he didn't pick up on either his cell phone or his home phone. Unlike her, he had a land line. He's probably working late, she thought. She hated to tell even a tiny lie, but she had to if she wanted to surprise him.

"I'm out Christmas shopping," she had said. "My cell phone battery is almost dead. By the time I get home, you'll be asleep. Talk to you in the morning." And then she closed by saying, "I love you, Duncan."

She knew he wouldn't be able to reach her when she was in the air and didn't want him to worry.

On the flight Flower was far too excited to close her eyes, just thinking that every second she was getting closer to Duncan and would finally see Branscombe for the first time. When she landed at Logan Airport at 6 A.M., and switched her cell phone back on, she was disappointed and surprised that Duncan hadn't left her a message. He left her messages all the time, even when he knew she wouldn't be able to pick up.

An hour and a half later, while she was waiting to board

the first bus to New Hampshire, she called him. He still didn't answer. Her heart began to sink. But he could be in the shower, she thought. She left a message to call her back. "I know you must think I'm crazy," she tried to joke. "It's 4:30 in the morning in California, but I'm wide awake. It just felt so strange not to talk to you last night. I'm going back to sleep, but if you get this, leave me a message." She turned off her phone. She knew she couldn't speak to him when she was on the bus, in case someone seated near her started to talk.

She had climbed aboard the bus to Concord, and once there, switched to the local bus to Branscombe. Now that she was approaching Duncan's town, she was starting to feel uneasy. She kept checking her messages, but he *still* hadn't tried to call her back.

Don't borrow trouble, she told herself. But what if Duncan didn't *want* to be surprised like this? He was so orderly and methodical. For her to just show up, when he's the type who would want everything to be perfect for her first visit, might not have been such a good idea after all.

As the bus passed miles of snow-covered countryside, Flower convinced herself that all would be well. Finally they passed a sign reading ENTERING BRANSCOMBE. I know I'm going to love it here, she thought. At the depot, she was the first one off the bus. She switched on her phone again. No messages. Her heart quickening, she went straight to the ladies' room to freshen up.

No wonder they call that flight the red-eye, she thought ruefully as she noticed how tired her eyes looked. She brushed her teeth, splashed water on her face, reapplied light makeup, and ran a comb through her hair. I certainly don't look my best, but I don't care, and I don't think Duncan will either.

She had gotten the address of Conklin's Market online and printed out the directions from the bus depot. The store was only a few blocks away. As she stepped out onto the street, she turned right. She knew that Main Street was in that direction. She began walking, enjoying the sound of the crusty snow as it crunched beneath her sneakers. At the corner, she paused. Main Street's quaint charm was everything she had imagined it would be. Old-fashioned street lamps, the row of tidy stores, and the small decorated Christmas trees lining the curb could have been on a postcard. Duncan had told her the trees would light up as Santa drove through town at the opening of the Festival. As she turned left, she smiled at the sight of a young woman lifting a baby from a stroller into a car seat. That's what I want to be doing before too long, Flower thought. She passed a drug store, a real estate agency, and then, across the street, she saw a man and a woman standing in front of a jewelry store, examining the display window. They must work there, she thought— neither one of them has a coat on. As she watched, they hurried back into the store. If Duncan *did* buy me a ring for

Christmas, is that where he got it? she wondered, and then again the nagging thought hit her—Why hasn't he called me?

Finally she reached Duncan's workplace. A little bigger than she had expected, it still had the look of a nineteenth-century general store. The exterior was painted red with black trim. A sign read CONKLIN'S MARKET—A WELCOME AWAITS YOU.

But when Flower walked through the door, the atmosphere was anything but welcoming. To her right, there were long lines at the registers, with cashiers yelling for price checks. It seemed to her that everyone in her line of vision was scowling.

Duncan had told her that produce aisles were always located on one side of a store or the other. There were no fruits or vegetables in the vicinity of the front door, so Flower started making her way past the rows of aisles to the far wall on the other side. I'll just say a quick hello and get the key to his house, she thought nervously. But when she turned the corner to the produce section, there was no sign of Duncan. A woman with a white stripe in her hair was yelling at a young kid who couldn't have been more than twenty. Apples were scattered all over the floor, some still rolling off in different directions.

"What happened here?" the woman screeched.

"I guess I piled the apples too high."

"I guess so! Pick them up, put them back, and unpack

the bananas. Look at those grapes! I told you to spray them, not drown them."

Oh, my goodness, Flower thought. She must be the owner's wife, the one they call The Skunk. But where was Duncan? Something had to be wrong.

The woman started to hurry past Flower.

"Excuse me," Flower said quickly. "Is Duncan Graham here?"

Her eyes shooting darts, the woman snarled, "You've got to be kidding. Where have you been, under a rock? He won millions in the lottery last night along with four other jokers who worked here. He'll never be back. Talk about ungrateful!"

In a huff, she was off.

Feeling as if she'd been punched in the stomach, Flower lowered her head as she felt tears flooding her eyes. Why didn't he call me? she asked herself frantically. The first thing I would have done if I had won the lottery, if I even played it, would be to call him. No matter what time it was, I would have called him. We phoned each other all the time over the silliest little things . . . And even if he thought my cell phone was dead, he knew it would have taken a message.

A stark realization hit her. He didn't call me because after he won the lottery, he probably thought he'd find someone better. My mother was right. She's laid-back about most things in life, but she warned me to take it slow with a man I met online who lives three thousand miles away . . .

"Flower," her mother had cautioned, "you haven't met his friends or family or visited his home yet. Just be careful."

The words of her late grandmother also echoed in her ears: "You should know someone for a year before getting serious."

She and Duncan had met only seven months ago.

I've made a fool of myself, Flower thought, as she squeezed past the shopping carts that were clustered around the cash registers. But I thought I knew him. He told me the other night that he wasn't going to play the lottery anymore. His financial advisers said it was a waste of money. What made him change his mind?

It was a relief to get out of the store. Flower knew if anyone looked at her closely, they'd see she was crying. I'm so tired, she realized as she shifted her knapsack on her shoulders and started walking toward the bus station. I may have to wait hours for a bus back to the airport. She noticed that an older woman eyed her sympathetically as they passed each other. I bet she's going to turn around and ask me if something's wrong, Flower thought. I've got to get off this Main Street. Ducking down an alley, she walked past a parking lot and found herself on a quiet country lane.

Across the street she could see a rambling white house with a sign that read THE HIDEAWAY — BED AND BREAKFAST. That's perfect, she thought. Just what I need. I can't get back on a bus yet. I need to just collapse and be alone.

She bit her lip, wiped her eyes, and hurried across the

road. Instructions on the front door said to ring the bell and walk in. I just hope they're not booked up, she thought, as she poked her finger on the bell, opened the door, and stepped into a small foyer. On the registration desk, an electrical smiling Santa was waving his arms and bowing. To the left, she could see a parlor with a large fireplace, comfortable looking couches, a crotcheted rug, and a huge Christmas tree, decorated with lights and ornaments and tinsel. The only sound was the ticking of a grandfather clock. Then she heard footsteps hurrying down the hall and a voice calling, "I'll get it, Jed."

A matronly looking woman, her graying hair pulled into a loose bun, was wiping her hands on an apron as she greeted Flower warmly. "Hello, honey. Here for the Festival?"

"Uhhhhh, yes. But I can only stay tonight."

"We happen to have one room left. It's nice and quiet and in the back. I have to warn you though. We have no television, radio, or Internet connection." She laughed. "Are you still interested?"

"More than ever," Flower said, managing a smile.

After handing over her credit card and driver's license, Flower detected the usual reaction to her name. "So you're from California," the woman said, not sounding surprised. She took an imprint of the credit card on an old machine, the likes of which Flower hadn't seen in years. "I'm Betty Elkins. My husband, Jed, and I are the owners here. Anything at all we can do to make you comfortable, please let us know. One of us is here all the time. We serve tea in the parlor at three o'clock with homemade scones and clotted cream." She paused. "You heard about our Festival all the way in California?"

"I did," Flower answered, thinking sadly of her conversations with Duncan. She could tell Betty Elkins was anxious to hear more, but thankfully a man appeared who was obviously Betty's husband. The sleeves of his green flannel shirt were rolled up, revealing muscular arms. He wore suspenders and a knotted bandana around his neck.

Betty glanced at him. "We've got a full house, honey," she said cheerfully, then turned back to Flower. "May I call you Flower?" she asked.

"Of course."

"Flower, this is my husband, Jed."

The gray-haired, thick eyebrowed Jed shook her hand. "I'm here to carry the luggage, but it looks like you don't have much except that knapsack."

"That's it," Flower said with a shrug as he matter-of-factly took the bag from her.

"Show her to the room, Jed. I've got to check on my Christmas cookies. They must be about ready."

Jed led Flower up the stairs and down the hall to a cozy room with yellow flowered wallpaper, a four-poster bed with a jonquil-patterned yellow quilt, a rocking chair, a night table, and a dresser. "This room is perfect for a girl with your name," he commented as he put the knapsack on the chair. "Hope you'll be comfortable."

"I know I will. Thank you." When Flower closed the door behind him, she turned the lock, took off her coat, sat down on the bed, and kicked off her sneakers.

I've never felt so alone, she thought. I truly believed Duncan loved me. But if he still wanted to be with me after winning all that money, he certainly would have called by now. She turned off her cell phone, leaned back onto the fluffy pillows, and immediately fell into a deep, dark sleep.

# 10

It was quarter of twelve when the four Reillys pulled into the driveway of the quaint, century-old Branscombe Inn. A half dozen television trucks were already lined up near the entrance.

"Looks like this press conference really drew the media," Nora commented.

"It sure does," Regan agreed. Her attention was riveted on a fortyish man, with a red face and balding head, dressed in jeans, boots, and a heavy parka, who was scowling and gesturing as he spoke on-camera to a reporter. "Look at that guy. I wonder what's on his mind. He certainly can't be one of the lottery winners."

"Maybe he is and just found out how much Uncle Sam is going to share in his winnings," Luke suggested.

Jack stopped the car at the front door. "I'll grab a luggage cart. Let's unload the bags and get inside. I know Steve and Muffy will be looking for us."

The Reillys had barely stepped into the noisy lobby when

they spotted their hosts across the room. "Such an attractive couple," Nora murmured. "That will certainly help on the campaign trail."

"You made it!" Muffy cried as she rushed over to them. Her shoulder-length blond hair was perfectly streaked and held back by a red-and-green striped headband. A whimsical sleigh-shaped pin was fastened to the lapel of her emerald-green suit.

Dark-haired, brown-eyed, Steve was right behind her, dressed in a pinstripe business suit, crisp white shirt, and a tie with the same pattern as Muffy's headband. "Hey, buddy, good to see you," he said to Jack, giving him an affectionate hug. His smile was quickly replaced by a worried frown, but he greeted the rest of the Reillys with genuine pleasure. "Hope you all had a good trip."

"Me, too," Muffy added quickly, getting the niceties out of the way. "Nora," she wailed, "you've *got* to help us get this Festival back on track. All anyone cares about is that stupid lottery. And that horrible producer Gary Walker not only cancelled our interview, but now he's trying to make the Festival and this town look foolish."

"We saw a man being interviewed outside who looked very upset," Nora began. "He had on a parka and jeans . . ."

"That's Harvey! His ex-wife, Glenda, is one of the winners. They were divorced about three months ago," Muffy explained.

"His ex-wife is now a multimillionaire?" Jack asked. "No

wonder he's not happy. I bet he wishes they had kissed and made up."

"Glenda doesn't," Steve said. "The guy's a jerk."

"What happened to the poor fellow who's missing?" Nora asked.

"Duncan Graham is still unaccounted for," Steve said. "Folks have been out looking for him all morning. But that producer is pushing the theory that Duncan was the one who bought the other winning ticket, then hightailed it out of here. Everyone in town is arguing about it and taking bets. The latest development is that the local jeweler is displaying a ring Duncan put a deposit on six months ago and was expected to pick up before Christmas. People are guessing that a girlfriend collected him, and they took off."

"Can you believe this happened just at the start of our Festival of Joy?" Muffy asked, her blue eyes widening. "I can't," she answered herself.

She is obviously going with the girlfriend theory, Regan thought.

"Listen," Steve said, looking around and lowering his voice. "There were so many reporters swarming into town this morning when word about the lottery broke that I thought it would be a good idea to call a press conference and let them get their pictures and stories all at once."

I'll bet it was Muffy's idea, Regan thought. One way or the other, she's going to get herself in front of the camera. She's not about to let those coordinating outfits go to waste.

"I'll open with a few remarks," Steve continued, "introduce the lottery winners, then, after they take questions, I'll switch the focus to the Festival and the fact that we have lots of wonderful things going on this weekend, like Nora Regan Reilly here to sign books."

The press is only interested in the lottery winners, Regan thought. Wait till Steve and Muffy find out they ended up on the cutting room floor.

"So, Nora, if you don't mind, after the reporters interview the lottery winners, I'll introduce you, then maybe you could say a few words about the Festival," Steve suggested.

"Of course," Nora said obligingly.

Steve beckoned to a clerk behind the desk. "These people are our guests—the Reillys," he said quickly. "Send their luggage up to their rooms please." He took Muffy's hand, and the Reillys followed him to a large parlor off the main lobby.

"Be careful of the wires," Steve warned as they entered the room. "They're all over the place."

Furniture had been pushed against the back wall. Rows of folding chairs were nearly filled. Cameras were directed at a table at the end of the room where two men and two women were seated. A fifth chair in the middle was empty.

"There are our winners," Steve said.

They look more exhausted than exhilarated, Regan thought as she observed them. She could see from the thin black wires on their lapels that they had already been miked.

The two men, one in his twenties and the other middle-aged, were whispering to each other. An older woman was trying to squash down the ruffles of a pink blouse that climbed halfway up her chin. But it was the obvious distress on the other woman's face that caught Regan's eye. She's *really* worried, Regan thought.

Steve brought the Reillys over to the table and quickly introduced them to the winners. Marion brightened immediately when she met Nora.

"Nora Regan Reilly. I *love* your books. You should write our story . . ."

Regan turned to Glenda. "I know you must be upset about your friend."

"I am," Glenda said.

"I'm a private investigator," Regan told her. "And my husband is the head of the Major Case Squad for the NYPD. We'd love to do whatever we can to help find him."

Glenda's eyes brightened. "Thank you. We were searching for Duncan all morning. Then we had to get ready for this press conference. We promised the mayor we'd be here."

"When did you first realize that he was missing?" Regan asked, wondering if Glenda knew her ex-husband was in the middle of a heart-to-heart interview with a reporter outside.

"I tried to call Duncan last night as soon as we won, but I couldn't reach him. This morning we stopped by his house at quarter of seven on our way to register the ticket, but he didn't answer the door. We thought he might have had a few too many beers and was sleeping it off. Last night we got stiffed on our Christmas bonus, and he was very upset when he left work. After we validated the ticket at the convenience store, we went back to his place and he *still* didn't answer the door. We kept ringing the bell and knocking on the windows. Finally, Tommy noticed the key ring in the ignition of his car. We decided to use his house key to go inside, just in case something happened to him. I felt funny just barging in there . . ."

"I would have done the same thing if I was concerned about a friend," Regan said. "The fact that the keys were in his car would have really worried me."

"That's the way I felt!" Glenda cleared her throat. "The television was on, the lights were on, his bed didn't look as though it had been slept in, there was no sign that he had taken a shower and gone out early . . ." Her voice trailed off. "Then we tried to start his car, but it was dead. I think that last night he must have realized our lottery numbers won. He was probably so frustrated that he hadn't played, he decided to go out, but his car wouldn't start. I think Duncan might have started walking and had an accident or a heart attack. I know he didn't buy that other lottery ticket!" she said, her eyes flashing. "But Tommy and Ralph think he's fine and would have been at work today if he hadn't come into money. They're furious with me because we announced his name as one of the winners of our ticket. If it ever turns out that Duncan cashes in the other winning ticket, I think they'll kill me. I'm the one who initially suggested cutting him in on the ticket, even though he was too cheap and stubborn to throw in a lousy dollar."

Oh boy, Regan thought. Alvirah better get here soon. She has at least four new candidates for the Lottery Winners Support Group.

Steve looked at his watch. "It's noon. We should get started." He gestured for the Reillys to take the seats he'd reserved for them in the front row, then went to the podium and pulled out a folded sheet of paper from his pocket. With Muffy at his side, he tapped on the microphone for silence.

"Welcome everyone, to Branscombe's first annual Festival of Joy. I am Mayor Steve Patton, and this is my wife, Muffy."

"Hi, everyone." Muffy giggled, leaning toward the mike. "I can't tell you what an honor and a pleasure and a delight it is for me to be the First Lady of Branscombe. Branscombe is such a special, special town. For those folks who don't live here, we want to welcome you, and we hope all of you are staying for the entire Festival of Joy. We promise you a wonderful, heartwarming experience . . ."

"Thank you, Muffy," Steve interrupted.

Muffy raised her index finger. "One more thing, honey. Tickets are still available for the community supper tomorrow night and the pancake breakfast Sunday morning. With the ticket you get a pass to see *It's a Wonderful Life,* which will be shown continually in the church auditorium. Don't you just love that movie? I cry every time I see it . . ."

Regan was amused by Steve's ability to keep smiling as he struggled to regain control of the microphone.

"I just love that movie, too," Steve said. "And now I want to introduce our lottery winners, who proved that Branscombe is not only a happy town, but a *lucky* town, a town where people care about each other and cheer each other's good fortune. That fifth seat is reserved for Duncan Graham, the coworker these folks so generously decided would share in that great big pot of money, even though, thanks to advice from his financial advisers, he decided not to play this week." Steve laughed. "I'd love to know what other kind of advice those guys are giving!"

"What are their names?" a reporter called out.

"Not sure," Steve answered. "We'll get you that information later. Now let me introduce the four recent employees of Conklin's Market, which, incidentally, will be catering the Festival."

As their names were called, the winners stood and waved. When they were all seated again, Steve turned to the audience. "I'd like to open up the floor to your questions."

Hands shot up. Steve pointed to a young woman in the second row.

"Is it true you left the framed photos that the Conklins gave you for Christmas outside the store this morning, tied together with a note saying, 'We Quit!'?" the woman asked, clutching her notebook.

"Yes, we did!" Marion said proudly. "That was my idea!"

"Did you think that was a nice way to start off the Festival of Joy?" another reporter called out. "We understand you are, or should I say were, their key employees. Wouldn't it have shown cooperation and good fellowship to work at Conklin's this weekend when they certainly must need your help catering the Festival?"

"It would have shown good fellowship to give us the Christmas bonus we had every right to expect," Ralph said hotly. "I can tell you one thing. We'd all be right there right now, millionaires or not, if they had treated us fairly."

Oh boy, Regan thought. The Festival of Joy is off to a great start.

Another reporter stood. "We understand your missing coworker made a down payment on a ring at Pettie's Fine Jewelry here in Branscombe six months ago. Do any of you know if he has a girlfriend?"

They all shook their heads.

"I see," the reporter said. "I must ask you. Do any of you think your coworker, or perhaps the intended recipient of this ring, bought the other winning lottery ticket?"

Ralph and Tommy both looked at each other, then raised their hands. "We do now," they said in unison.

Marion looked perplexed. She bit her lip, then fluttered her hands, indicating she couldn't make up her mind.

Glenda jumped to her feet. "No!" she said vehemently. "He wouldn't have betrayed us like that. I'm terribly afraid something happened to him."

"Something did!" Duncan cried from the back of the room.

The crowd gasped and turned to see a disheveled, unshaven Duncan hobbling toward the microphone, his right hand wrapped around a splintery-looking wooden pole. "I am outraged that anyone, especially Tommy and Ralph, would think that I would go out and buy a ticket behind my friends' backs!" he shouted. "I did NOT buy that other ticket! I swear on my life I didn't!" His voice was quivering as he reached the podium and turned to face the crowd.

"I knew it, Duncan!" Glenda cried.

"And even worse! That special moment in a man's life when he pops the question to his girlfriend has been ruined for me! I find it disgusting that the jeweler in this town would invade my privacy for his own profit!"

With that ringing statement, Duncan, weakened by fatigue, hunger, and pain, collapsed into the arms of Mayor Steve.

# 11

An hour into their drive to Boston, Edmund and Woodrow were still bursting with excitement at their incredible stroke of luck.

Woodrow was at the wheel of their rented sedan. "Dark gray, nothing flashy," they had told the agent at Budget Rent A Car. Each of them owned a top of the line Mercedes, but that was not the image of economy and thrift they wanted to convey to their clients.

They took turns coming up with new ways to describe their winnings.

"180 million beans!" Woodrow said.

"180 million big ones!" Edmund countered.

"180 million smackers!" Woodrow chortled.

From time to time ever-cautious Edmund would remind Woodrow to slow down. "We could hit an ice patch and get in an accident. We have too much to live for."

"I have a perfect driving record," Woodrow insisted.

"Too bad you have another record," Edmund said dryly.

Woodrow laughed. "Talk about the pot calling the kettle black. Yours is just as long as mine. Thank God, we can be squeaky-clean from now on. But I'm going to *miss* cheating people."

"Me, too. But it's not worth it. That judge threatened to lock us up and throw away the key if we ever got caught in another swindle."

"I wish we didn't have to go back to Branscombe for the final session."

"You think it's my idea of a good time? But if we're not there for the class, our students might start comparing notes. This way we'll say our individual good-byes to them and promise a weekly report on the oil well until we cash the ticket and disappear."

Woodrow was silent for a moment, then said, "Edmund, I have an idea."

"I'm listening."

"We paid our dues for the other scams. Why not wipe the slate clean? Why don't we return the money to the people in Branscombe next week? We don't need it now. We'll tell them the oil well is not as secure as we were led to believe but promise to keep in touch about future investments we think are worth considering. That way we won't have to worry ever again about having the Feds on our tail."

Edmund frowned. "Give people back their money? How

unnatural." He pretended to shiver. "It goes against my every instinct. Besides, we worked hard convincing them to cough up that dough."

"Eddie, it's chump change now. Sixteen of our seventeen students invested in the greasy driveway we called an oil well. How much did we collect? Seventy-one thousand dollars? I'll tell you one person who will be thrilled to get his money back—Mr. Duncan Donuts. Maybe he'll go back to buying lottery tickets."

"He must be really out of his mind mad at us right now," Edmund laughed.

"I hope he doesn't show up for class next week," Woodrow said. "He might kill us."

"I thought you wanted to pay him back."

"We can send him a check."

Edmund's eyes twinkled. "Woodrow, what are we going to do with ourselves when we collect all that money?"

"Have fun, that's what we're going to do."

"Together, right."

"Of course, together. We're a winning team. We'll always stick together."

Edmund shifted nervously in his seat. "So you think Aunt Millie is the right person to cash in our ticket?"

"She's perfect," Woodrow answered. "She's the one person in our family who always loved us unconditionally, no matter how much trouble we got in. She has no heirs but us, thank God, so she won't have anyone telling her to keep all our money. We'll give her a million bucks to make the trip to lottery headquarters." He laughed. "You know her. She'll love the excitement."

"I just hope she doesn't have a criminal record she hasn't told us about," Edmund joked.

Woodrow laughed. "Can you imagine that? Aunt Millie forbidden to gamble?"

"If that's the case, she's broken parole at least a thousand times. She turns into a demon when she sits in front of those slot machines in Atlantic City. Can you believe how mad she got when they started computerizing those one-armed bandits? She said half the fun is hearing the sound of quarters tumbling into her bucket. Clink, clink."

"We sure take after her more than either one of our mothers," Woodrow said. "I just hope we can trust her to do right by us." He paused. "That wasn't nice. I know we can. We'll pay her a surprise visit next week after we leave Branscombe in the dust."

Edmund leaned forward to turn up the heat. "It must be getting colder out," he observed. "But at least it's not snowing." He pushed the power button on the radio.

"This is station WXY in Boston. We have breaking news from our reporter in Branscombe, New Hampshire, covering the incredible lottery story. What have you got for us, Ginger?"

"Bob, we *do* have quite a story going on up here. The missing man, Duncan Graham, who was cut in on the lottery winnings by his generous coworkers even though he decided not to play last night . . ."

Woodrow whistled. "Way to go, Duncan! But he's missing?" He leaned over and turned up the volume.

". . . arrived just moments ago at the Branscombe Inn, where a press conference with his coworkers is taking place. He looks as if he's been through the ringer. He was angry and upset when he heard that two of his coworkers thought he had bought the other winning ticket behind their backs."

"He didn't," Woodrow and Edmund said in unison.

"He must have had some sort of accident because he limped to the podium, grabbing an old pole for support, a pole that looked as if he had fished it out of a Dumpster. He vehemently denied buying the other winning ticket, but, incredibly, he seemed more furious about the fact that the whole town knows about the engagement ring he bought for his girlfriend. He was so overwhelmed that he literally fainted at the podium!"

"He fainted?" Bob answered with appropriate concern in his voice. "Is he all right?"

"They're just carrying him out now. I'll keep you posted."

"Does he realize that his coworkers have cut him in on the winning ticket and that he's now worth twelve million dollars?"

"Hard to say."

"If he doesn't know, it'll be a nice surprise for him when he wakes up. Thanks, Ginger. And now to the weather . . ."

Woodrow and Edmund looked at each other.

"That gets us off the hook with Duncan," Edmund laughed. "He didn't lose out by following our advice. His coworkers must be crazy. They're cutting him in on millions. We'd never do that."

"We certainly wouldn't," Woodrow agreed.

"But what a shame we're out of the business of scamming people. We could have found some more oil wells for him."

Woodrow slapped his thigh and laughed. "You're right, Edmund. We would have ended up with at least eleven of his twelve million." He tapped on the brake. Construction ahead was reducing the traffic to a crawl.

Edmund shook his head. "Speaking about that ticket makes me want to feast my eyes on it again," he said as he retrieved his wallet from the breast pocket of his suit jacket. Smiling with anticipation, he pulled out the plastic bag and reached inside for the ticket.

Woodrow glanced over. "That sweet little piece of paper is worth 180 million bucks."

"That's right," Edmund said as he unfolded the ticket and looked at the numbers. A feeling of sheer panic raced through his system, a feeling he had never experienced before, not even when he was sentenced to eight years in prison. A moan escaped his lips.

"What's the matter?" Woodrow snapped.

"These numbers . . . they don't look right. I thought . . . I thought the Powerball number was 32."

"What?" Woodrow demanded.

"Wasn't the Powerball number 32?"

"Yes it was!"

"This Powerball number is 18 . . ."

"What are you talking about?" Woodrow screamed.

A bloodcurdling, anguished howl escaped Edmund's lips. "The date on this is June twelfth!" he screamed. "This is an old ticket! This is not our winning ticket! Oh, God, no!"

Woodrow grabbed it from him. "Are you trying to pull something on me?"

"How dare you say that? How dare you? We checked the numbers when we put it in the freezer. But we didn't check them when we went back for it. Someone must have switched the tickets! You're an idiot! I knew we shouldn't have left the ticket behind! I knew it!"

"Who could have come in the house? We made sure it was all locked up! And we weren't gone for that long!"

"Remember last night we thought we heard a noise in the basement but didn't bother to check? We were too busy celebrating and thought it was the old furnace . . ."

Woodrow's eyes were bulging out of his head. "We heard that thumping noise. I wanted to check but you said not to bother." He pointed at the radio. "They said Duncan was missing last night. He just turned up, and he's limping. That stupid side door our students use was always unlocked." He looked back at Edmund. "I bet he came over to yell at us when he realized the numbers he didn't play won! He must have heard us celebrating! He spied on us!" He must have heard us talking about the oil well scam!

"It's *got* to be him!" Edmund screamed. "Who else could it be?"

His temples throbbing, his face beet red, Woodrow gunned the car across the grassy median and made a highly illegal U-turn. "We're going to get that ticket back!"

"What if he already called the cops on us?"

"I don't care!" Woodrow exploded.

Edmund slumped in his seat. "It amazes me that you have a perfect driving record."

# 12

Up in the clouds above New Hampshire, Willy glanced out the window of the twin-engine jet he and Alvirah had chartered at Westchester Airport. This is the last thing I expected to be doing today, he thought, then looked across the aisle at Alvirah, who was smiling gleefully. She reached out her hand to him.

"When we heard about that oil spill on the Connecticut Turnpike, wasn't it an inspiration for me to call Rent A Jet?"

"Expensive inspiration," Willy commented. "We save a few hours on the road, and it costs us three thousand bucks."

"All that driving would have been too much for you."

"Alvirah, I love to drive."

Dramatically, she touched the bandage on her forehead. "When I was little and I got hurt, my mother always gave me a present. After I broke my arm running down a slide, she bought me a new Dy-dee doll, with two matching outfits. It made me feel so much better. She wasn't even mad at me for being so stupid. This plane ride is my get-well present to my-self. Besides, it's okay to splurge on ourselves once in a while."

"You're right, Alvirah."

"And something else. I'm worried about those lottery winners. They look as if they need my help. If we were in the car, we wouldn't get there until tonight."

It was now 12:15, and they were beginning their descent into the small local airport, ten miles from Branscombe.

Alvirah finished the last of the tiny twist pretzels she had been munching on during the flight. "They were stale," she whispered to Willy as she crumbled the bag. "But I was hungry."

The pilot had called ahead and arranged for a car service to pick them up and take them to the Branscombe Inn. When they landed, a white stretch limo was waiting on the tarmac.

"I'm Charley," the driver said as he loaded their bags into his trunk. "Welcome to the Festival of Joy."

"Have they found the guy who's missing?" Alvirah asked eagerly.

"Oh, you know about him?"

"She knows about *everything*," Willy explained.

Charley closed the trunk. "He just limped into a press conference a few minutes ago, denied he bought the other winning ticket, then keeled over. I guess he'll be okay, but he had some kind of wild night, that's for sure."

Alvirah's eyes widened. "Do you think he bought that other ticket?"

"Who knows? As a matter of fact, I just passed the place where it was sold."

"Where?"

"A little convenience store down the road."

"The pretzels on the plane made me thirsty. Let's stop there for water."

"Don't worry. I have plenty of bottled water in the car for my guests," Charley said as he opened the door for them.

Alvirah shivered as she climbed into the back of the limo. "You know something? I'm cold. What I really need is a cup of coffee."

"There's a coffee shop along the way that serves the best . . ." Charley began.

"Don't waste your breath," Willy interrupted. "Nothing is going to stop my wife from checking out that convenience store."

"Gotcha," Charley said as he closed the door behind them.

# 13

Someone call an ambulance!" Mayor Steve shouted, as he lowered Duncan to the floor and unzipped his parka.

"I know what to do!" Muffy cried. "I was a lifeguard!" Dropping to her knees, she grabbed Duncan's wrist and felt for his pulse. "His heart is still beating!" she announced dramatically.

Regan and Jack had been the first to spring from their chairs. "Muffy, see if he has a medical alert card in his wallet," Regan suggested.

Duncan's eyes flew open. "I'm okay!" he insisted. "I have no medical conditions. None whatsoever." Cameras clicked nonstop as he tried to sit up. "Please! I'm fine. My leg hurts, that's all."

Glenda rushed to his side as photographers and reporters jostled for a good vantage point to catch the action. "Please stand back," she urged, then looked at Steve. "Let's get Duncan out of here."

Jack and Steve lifted Duncan onto a chair, picked it up, and hurried him out of the parlor.

The hotel manager led the way to a guest room down the hall. "When the ambulance comes, I'll send the paramedics in," he said.

"I'll be all right," Duncan insisted. "My leg might need to be X-rayed. I'm thirsty and hungry and I want to call my girlfriend. Glenda, can I borrow your cell phone? I left mine home," he said as Jack and Steve set down the chair and eased him onto the bed.

"I have it right here, Duncan. What's her number?"

Duncan rattled it off then grabbed the phone from Glenda's hand and held it to his ear. "Her voice mail is picking up," he said, his tone frustrated and disappointed, then he dropped his voice. "Flower, I love you. I need to talk to you. I don't have my cell phone with me . . ."

"Tell her to call mine," Glenda said quickly, then gave him her number.

Duncan repeated it into the phone. "I'll try you at work, Flower. I can't wait to talk to you." He hung up. "Glenda, do you mind if I call information? There's a charge for it."

Glenda smiled. "Don't you realize I'm now a multi-millionaire? And you are, too, Duncan."

"Must be nice," Mayor Steve said as he handed Duncan the glass of water he'd hurried to fill.

"I heard. No one ever had a better friend than you,

Glenda," Duncan said humbly. He then gulped every drop in the glass. "You're the best."

"That's for sure," Jack said with a laugh. "I doubt if I'll ever make friends with someone who's willing to share their millions with me."

Duncan reached the day care center but frowned when he was told by Flower's boss that she had taken the day off. "She *did*? I'm surprised she didn't tell me. Okay then, I'll wait to hear back from her."

He hung up and then called and picked up the voice messages on his home and cell phones, smiling as he listened. "Aw, she couldn't sleep last night," he said softly. "I hope she calls me back soon." He then dialed his parents and left a message. As he gave Glenda back her phone, he looked at Jack and Steve. "Thanks, guys. Please don't let me hold you up. I'll be fine here until the ambulance comes."

"How did you hurt that leg?" Jack asked.

"I fell," Duncan said quickly. "I'll be okay. Thanks again for your help. If you don't mind, I'd just like to have a word with Glenda."

"I'm going to the hospital with you," Glenda said firmly. "You shouldn't be alone."

"Glenda, I can't believe that Tommy and Ralph would think . . ." A look of distress came over Duncan's face.

"We'll step outside and let you two talk," Jack said. He and Steve went out into the hallway where the other Reillys were waiting.

"Glenda!" Duncan whispered when they were alone. "I need to tell you something!"

An alarmed look crossed Glenda's face. "Duncan, please don't say you bought that other ticket."

"No! I didn't. But my life could be in danger . . ."

"What are you *talking* about?"

Duncan quickly recounted the events of the previous evening. ". . . so take a look at this," he said hoarsely. He reached into the side pocket of his parka and pulled out his wallet.

Glenda looked dumbfounded as she took the lottery ticket from his hand and checked the numbers. "You *stole* this out of their freezer?"

"Yes! I can never cash it in, but I don't want them to have it. All I care about is getting those two arrested for swindling innocent people out of their hard-earned money. If I ever cashed this, they'd know it was me who stole it, and I'd never be able to sleep at night without worrying they'd someday climb in my bedroom window and kill me. Besides, people around here would always think I might have intended to double-cross you, even though I'd split the winnings."

"You know if you hadn't told those guys our numbers in the first place, we'd be sharing the whole pot," she said wryly.

"I'm sorry! Don't forget it was my Powerball number that won."

"I was joking, Duncan."

"You know, Glenda, the more I think about it, the more I

believe they're not just swindlers—they're dangerous!" From outside they could hear the wail of an approaching ambulance. "What should I do now?"

Glenda pointed in the direction of the hallway. "That guy who just carried you in with the Mayor? He's the head of the NYPD Major Case Squad, and his wife's a private investigator. Before you showed up, she offered their help in looking for you. Why don't you talk to them?"

"You think they can be trusted to keep quiet about the ticket and get those crooks arrested?"

"Yes, I do, Duncan."

Muffy, the former lifeguard, came barging in the room with a breakfast tray, a camera crew close on her heels. "Duncan, our wonderful volunteer ambulance workers are right behind me. But have a few bites of a delicious, homemade waffle before you go."

Glenda had instinctively closed her hand around the lottery ticket. Now she looked at Duncan, her eyes questioning.

"Glenda," he said, gesturing toward her hand. "Why don't you follow up on that, then meet me at the hospital with my cell phone?"

"Follow up on what?" Muffy asked brightly as two men in white uniforms, the seal of Branscombe over their hearts, wheeled a stretcher into the room.

# 14

Charley drove his limo past the solitary gas pump in front of Ethan's Convenience Store and stopped. A banner in the window proclaimed: A MEGA-MEGA LOTTERY TICKET WORTH $180 MILLION WAS SOLD HERE!

Alvirah, Willy close behind, was inside the store before Charley could even think about opening the door for them. A cameraman and a young male reporter came rushing toward them.

"I'm Jonathan Tuttle from the BUZ network," the reporter said excitedly. "I bet you two have the winning lottery ticket. Showing up in a limo and all . . ."

"Sorry to disappoint you," Alvirah said. As the cameraman snapped off his light and the reporter lowered his mike, she added breezily, "But we did win 40 million dollars in the lottery several years ago."

"Turn the camera back on," Tuttle ordered, then focused on Alvirah and Willy with renewed interest. "Wait a minute. Haven't you been interviewed on our network?"

"Yes, I'm Alvirah Meehan, and this is my husband, Willy. Your anchor Cliff Bailey has had me on whenever there are new lottery winners making headlines."

"Of course," Tuttle said. "What brings you up here?"

"We just flew in for Branscombe's Festival of Joy."

"Our network is doing a special on the Festival."

"I saw that this morning."

"Are you aware that two winning mega-mega lottery tickets were sold in this area, one here in Red Oak and one in Branscombe?"

"Yes we are. I hope to meet the winners in Branscombe and congratulate them personally."

"Do you have any advice for them?"

"Tell them to turn off their phones," Willy grunted.

Alvirah laughed. "What he means is that they'll hear from an awful lot of people with crazy ideas about how they should spend their money."

"I can imagine," Tuttle said. "Thank you Mrs. Meehan."

Alvirah glanced around the store. On the back wall hung a cardboard cutout of Santa and his reindeer landing on a rooftop. Bright red ornaments hung from a fake tree perched atop a table in the corner. Blinking Christmas lights framed the dairy section.

A peppy octogenarian in a plaid shirt and red bow tie was

behind the counter by the cash register. "What can I do for you folks?" he asked.

"We'll have two large black coffees to go, please," Alvirah said.

"You got it."

"Are you Ethan?" she asked.

"Sure am."

"How exciting that you sold one of the winning lottery tickets," Alvirah commented as he poured the coffee.

"Sure is. It's the first time! I get a check, too, because it was bought here. That'll be a nice piece of change for me. But before you ask, I'll answer the questions everyone's been calling me with all morning. I don't know who bought it and I don't have security cameras so there are no tapes to play over and over. As far as that guy they think might have bought it, I have no idea. I don't know what he looks like, and even if I *did* see a picture of him, it wouldn't make any difference. If he's not one of my regular customers, I won't remember."

Alvirah nodded her head. "That answers all my questions."

Ethan laughed as he emphatically secured caps onto the cardboard coffee cups. "Maybe it's my age, but after a while all the people in and out of here become a blur. Yesterday it seemed that everyone who bought gas splurged on a ticket. I was busier than a one-armed paper hanger."

"When the pot gets that big," Willy said, "people want to get in on the dream. Winning the lottery certainly changed our life. Alvirah, do you want anything else besides the coffee?"

"I wouldn't mind something to munch on," Alvirah answered as she looked around the countertop that was cluttered with packages of gum, candy, and donuts. Her eyes stopped at a basket of Christmas caramels, individually wrapped in red and green striped tin foil.

"Are these caramels any good?" Alvirah asked Ethan.

"For a dollar a piece, they'd better be. I just got them in the other day." He shrugged. "I had a couple myself. They're delicious. But more people with an extra buck spent it on a lottery ticket than one of those."

"We'll take a dozen," Willy said, then looked at Alvirah. "They're my get-well present to you."

# 15

Flower awoke with a start. She had been dreaming that she was hanging from a ledge, trying to pull herself up. Her fingers were slipping, and she was trying to call for help, but no sound would come out of her mouth. She quickly opened her eyes and saw the unfamiliar pattern of the flowered wallpaper. Where am I? she asked herself. Still frightened by the dream, she was grateful to be awake, then the crushing realization of where she was and why she was there set in.

With a heavy heart she glanced at her watch. It was ten after one. I've only been asleep for a few hours, she realized. But I'm hungry, and I'm getting a headache. Betty and Jed had said to let them know if I wanted anything. Maybe I can grab a sandwich and a cup of tea, then I'll call and see if I can catch a flight back tonight. Her cell phone was on the dresser. I don't want to turn it on yet, she thought. Even if there was a message from Duncan, I don't want to listen to his lame excuses or a suggestion that we'd be better off just being friends.

She went into the small bathroom and splashed water on

her face. If things were different, I wouldn't have minded taking a long soak in that claw-foot tub, she thought, envisioning her mother at home, lolling in her bath with layers of seaweed floating around her.

"It's so soothing, Flower," her mother would say, as she sniffed the aroma of the lavender candles that inevitably were part of the ritual. "I can't believe you're not into this."

From the time I was a little kid, I was more than content with hot water and plain soap, Flower thought. Just like Nana, who said the only place seaweed belonged was on the beach, not clogging the drains. She sighed. It had been six years, and she still missed Nana so much.

Enough reminiscing Flower decided, suddenly restless. I want to get something to eat, take a quick shower, and get out of here.

When she left the room there was no sound in the hallway except the creaking of the floorboards under her feet. Betty had said they had a full house, but it didn't seem as if there was anyone around now. She walked downstairs to the first floor.

There was no one at the desk in the foyer, and she could see that the parlor was empty. But the air was filled with the enticing smell of baking—chocolate cake. Betty's last name should be Crocker, Flower thought, as she walked to the back of the house and knocked on the kitchen door.

"Yooooou hooooo!" Betty called. "Whoever you are, come on in!"

"It's me," Flower said as she pushed the swinging door open and stepped into a large, old-fashioned kitchen. At the far end a fire was blazing in the hearth, two inviting looking club chairs in front of it. Shiny copper pots and pans hung from the ceiling. Checkered curtains framed the large windows on either side of the back door. Through them Flower could see a small red building that looked like an old barn.

Betty was leaning over the oven, examining the toothpick in her right hand. The look on her face was one of intense concentration. "Be right with you, Flower," she said cheerily. "I like my cakes to come out just perfectly. A minute more and this one would start to be a teeny weeny bit dry. I always say, timing is everything." She lifted the baking pan out of the oven and set it on a rack on the side of the stove.

"If it tastes as good as it smells, I'm sure it's perfect," Flower said softly.

Betty turned to her with a big smile. "I'm my own best customer," she said, wiping her broad hands on her apron. "That's why I'll never be a Skinny Minnie. Hey, I'm surprised to see you. You looked so tired when you came in, I was sure you'd sleep for hours."

"I thought I would too, but I guess I woke up because I'm hungry. Would it be possible to get a little something to eat?"

"Of course, honey. Jed and I just had some of my fresh vegetable soup for lunch. Would you like a bowl of that with a nice warm biscuit?"

"I'd love it."

"Okay, then. Would you like to have it right here or perhaps you'd prefer to take it up to your room?"

Betty's friendliness made Flower feel less alone. "Right here, if I won't be in your way."

"You won't be in my way. I love it when our guests drop into the kitchen and we get a chance to visit. You look a little peaked. Why don't you sit down?" she asked, indicating the somewhat battered wooden table.

Five minutes later, Flower was gratefully sipping the soup, and Betty, a cup of tea in hand, had settled in the chair across from her.

"This soup is delicious," Flower said quietly.

"Makes me feel good to see people enjoy my cooking," Betty replied amiably, then sipped her tea. "So the Festival of Joy is finally here. Everyone's been talking about it for months. We have TV people covering the Festival staying here. Are you going to the candlelight ceremony tonight, dear?"

Flower burst into tears.

"I didn't think so," Betty said sympathetically, her motherly face benevolent. "Is this about a man?"

"Yes," Flower said, wiping her eyes. She felt her nose begin to run.

Betty reached in her pocket and took out a packet of tissues. "Oh, my dear," she clucked as she handed them to Flower.

"I'm sorry," Flower apologized as she dabbed at her eyes and blew her nose.

"No need to be sorry. You're such a sweet, pretty girl. Whoever is making you cry is not worth even one of those tears." She reached across the table and enveloped Flower's small hand in hers. "Would it help to talk about it?"

Flower nodded and put down her spoon. "My boyfriend, or I should say my *ex*-boyfriend, lives in Branscombe. I flew in to surprise him for the weekend. This morning I went over to Conklin's Market where he works and found out that he and a group of coworkers had won . . . won . . . won the lottery last night!" She started crying even harder, gasping for breath as she said, "He didn't even call me to tell me. Since last June we spoke at least twice a day and always at night. Last night he didn't call. I left him messages, and he never called me back, not even this morning. I know it means that now that he has money, he wants to be able to live it up without me!"

"Well for land's sake," Betty exclaimed. "He sounds *awful*." She leaned forward. "Some of the workers at Conklin's won the lottery?"

Flower hiccupped. "Yes."

"Who's your boyfriend?"

"Duncan Graham. He runs the produce section."

"Duncan? I'm so surprised, I thought he was a lovely fellow."

A fresh torrent of tears flowed from Flower's eyes, and she began to sob.

"I'm so sorry," Betty said as she got up, went around the table, and pulled Flower's head to her generous bosom. "That was a stupid thing for me to say. If he treated you like that, you're well rid of him. Who did you talk to at the store?"

"I think . . . I think . . . it was Mr. Conklin's wife. She wasn't very nice."

"She's a horrible woman! Nasty as they come." Betty soothingly patted Flower's head.

"I just want to go home," Flower said, weeping. "I'll get a bus to Boston today."

"Are you sure you don't want to spend the night? You can have dinner with me and Jed. Then you can get a fresh start in the morning."

"I don't know," Flower answered uncertainly. "I think I'm better off just leaving here as fast as I can." She looked up into Betty's eyes. "The thing is that Duncan's been taking a financial course with two guys who came to Branscombe last month. He told me they advised him to stop playing the lottery, and he agreed it wasn't a good idea anymore. He obviously didn't listen to them. I wish he had!"

"No you don't!" Betty cried. "He's shown his true colors. If you ask me, you dodged a bullet, honey. Even if he had all the money in the world, he doesn't deserve you."

"Those two financial advisers will really come in handy now. They can tell him what to do with all his winnings," Flower said, sounding forlorn. "Have you heard anything about them? Woodrow and Edmund Winthrop. They're cousins."

"Not a thing," Betty said quickly. "And if I had, I wouldn't have been interested. Money is the ruination of so many people. As they say, it can't buy you happiness. You're going to go back to California and find someone wonderful, I just know it. Jed and I will come to your wedding out there."

"I never met anyone kinder than you," Flower said, trying to smile.

A sharp rapping at the back door made them both jump. "I don't know who that could be," Betty murmured as she released Flower and hurried to answer it. She gasped when she saw who was on the porch. "It's not a good time to stop in," Betty said, her tone firm. Her hand was on the door. She started to close it.

From where Flower was sitting she couldn't see who the unwelcome visitor was.

"What are you talking about, Betty?" a man's voice asked angrily. "We've got a big problem, and we need to stay here. The cops may be looking for us at our place."

"You're always making jokes," Betty said nervously as she struggled to push the door closed.

Flower jumped up.

"Listen, Betty, Woodrow and I were there for you when

you and Jed needed to disappear," another man's voice snapped, his tone low but fiercely angry. "Where is he now? Out in the back duplicating keys of the poor dopes staying here so he can break into their homes?"

A second later Betty stumbled back as the door was shoved open and two men burst into the room. I've got to get out of here, Flower thought, as the intruders caught sight of her, their expressions shocked. Betty's head spun toward her, the look on her once-kindly face now terrifying. Flower turned and started to run out of the kitchen. Before she could reach the door, a heavy arm snapped around her waist, a firm hand covered her mouth, and she felt herself being swung around.

"Now what?" Betty asked Woodrow and Edmund bitterly, as she maintained a smothering grip over Flower's mouth.

# 16

The Reillys watched as Duncan was wheeled out of the room. The lottery winners had joined them in the hallway.

"Good luck, Duncan," Marion said, briefly touching his hand. "You have to be up and around by Monday so you can ride with us to Lottery Headquarters and officially turn in the ticket. Charley's driving us—we're going to make a day of it."

"Thanks, Marion," Duncan replied wanly.

Tommy and Ralph patted him on the shoulder but said nothing.

They're still not sure about him, Glenda thought. I can only imagine what they'd think if they knew I had the other ticket in my pocket. I can't believe I have both tickets on me right now.

The hotel manager came over to the group. "We're setting up a table in one of our private dining rooms. Please be our guests for a luncheon—relax and enjoy each other."

"That sounds delightful," Marion said. "Right now we'd be on our lunch break at Conklin's!" She turned to Nora. "You will join us, won't you?"

"We'd love to," Nora answered as she and Marion fell in step together.

Glenda tapped Regan's arm as the group moved down the hallway. "I need to speak to you for a moment. It's terribly important."

Regan nodded and stopped. Jack was walking ahead with Mayor Steve and Luke. Muffy had accompanied the stretcher out to the ambulance with the camera crew following. "Of course. What's wrong?"

Glenda looked around to be sure there was no one in earshot. "Duncan's in trouble . . ."

Regan listened as Glenda filled her in.

". . . so Duncan took a big risk by stealing their ticket. But he really wants them to be punished for what they've done to so many people. We need to get those two crooks behind bars as soon as possible."

"We need evidence of their scam before they can be arrested," Regan explained. "Do you know if they gave Duncan any paperwork when he made that investment?"

"I don't know. But I told him I'd go to his house to get his cell phone. This morning I noticed his notes from the financial course were on the dining room table."

"That's a start," Regan said. "I'll get Jack and the three of us will go over to Duncan's right away."

"I'm so lucky you're here, Regan. Thank you. But what excuse can we give for leaving now? We're supposed to stay for lunch."

"You want to deliver Duncan his cell phone. He hasn't been able to talk to his fiancée yet, and he's upset. He might be in the hospital for hours so he asked you to pick up his ring before the jeweler closes." Regan paused. "I hate to ask you this, Glenda, but did you know your ex was outside talking to the press?"

"It doesn't surprise me," Glenda said stoically.

Regan smiled. "It's actually good for us. He looked pretty upset. That gives Jack and me the perfect excuse for going with you. You shouldn't be alone."

Glenda smiled. "Great! If Harvey knew he was doing me a favor by mouthing off to reporters, he'd drop dead."

They walked into the dining room where their group was about to take seats at the table. Regan spoke quietly to Jack while Glenda talked to the others. Tommy's parents had joined the group and so had Ralph's wife, Judy.

"I wish you didn't have to leave!" Marion said. "But I understand about poor Duncan. Glenda, what about us all going to the bank to put our ticket in a safe deposit box for the weekend?"

"You guys go ahead and do that this afternoon. I trust you" she said, giving a look to Ralph and Tommy.

"Trust us?" Ralph joked. "Glenda, tell us. What happened to Duncan last night? How did he get hurt?"

"He fell," Glenda answered. "As you can imagine, he was pretty upset when he heard the winning numbers and he hadn't played. His car wouldn't start, he went for a walk and slipped. He never dreamt we'd be generous enough to share the money with him. I'm sure you've heard about the poor guy who always played the lottery with his friends at work. One day he was out sick and wasn't there to throw in his share. They won and didn't cut him in."

"That's so mean!" Marion exclaimed, then added, "Where was Duncan going? Does his girlfriend live in town?"

"No, she lives in California."

"I can't *wait* to meet her," Marion said. "Maybe she lives near my grandson. What's her name?"

"Flower."

"What?" Marion asked, squinting.

"Flower."

"How does she spell it?" Luke murmured to Nora.

"I see," Marion said. "I hope she likes the ring."

"I'm sure she will. Regan and Jack Reilly are nice enough to offer to come with me. They saw Harvey outside, looking pretty angry." She then joked, "Marion, you said we might need bodyguards. I've got two of them."

Two waiters came in the room, pads in hand, ready to take orders.

"Get going then," Marion chirped. "But don't forget to leave us that ticket."

Which one, Glenda thought wryly, as the whole room

watched her retrieve their winning ticket from her wallet and hand it over to Ralph. She could almost feel Duncan's ticket in her right pocket. I'm going to have a heart attack, she thought.

Regan could tell that her mother's antenna was up. She knows there's something else going on. It's going to kill her, but she'll have to wait until later to find out.

"I'll pull the car up while you two wait inside," Jack offered as he, Regan, and Glenda walked out of the dining room toward the reception area. "Glenda, if your ex is still hanging around, hopefully we can avoid him."

"Regan! Jack! There you are!" Alvirah's voice carried across the lobby. She and Willy were checking in at the front desk.

"Hi, Alvirah!" Regan called, waving her hand. "You got here fast!"

"Is that Alvirah Meehan?" Glenda whispered to Regan.

"Yes," Regan said. "My poor mother was wondering why we were leaving before lunch and was dying to find out. Trying to get out of here without Alvirah realizing that something's up will be a real challenge. She'll definitely want to come with us."

Glenda paused. "I've read about the cases she's solved. And she has always been so caring about her fellow lottery winners who've fallen into trouble. I trust her, and I'm sure Duncan would. If she wants to join us, let's bring her along."

"Believe me," Regan said. "I know Alvirah. She'll want to."

# 17

Sam Conklin rushed into his small office in the back of the store and slammed the door behind him. At that precise moment the phone rang. It was Richard, his only son, whom he had hoped would go into the family business. Instead, the smell of the greasepaint and the roar of the crowd had been an irresistible draw, and at forty-two, Richard was an established actor. He had just finished a nine-month run of a play in Boston and would soon be heading back to his apartment in New York.

"Dad, what's going on up there? It's all over the news about the lottery winners from Conklin's. They must have gotten the story wrong that you didn't give bonuses. That can't be true. You've always given bonuses and were always more than generous."

Sam sank into a chair and leaned his head on his hand. "It's true," he admitted miserably. "Rhoda talked me into it."

"Why doesn't that surprise me?" Richard asked quietly. "I can't stand that woman."

"Neither can I," Sam admitted.

"That's music to my ears," Richard said, his voice suddenly cheerful. "She's been nothing but trouble since Day One. When you think of how sweet Mom was . . ."

"I know, I know," Sam interrupted. "This morning has been a public relations nightmare. I've worked hard in this store for more than forty years and as you just said have always been generous to my employees. I'm so ashamed that I let her talk me into giving pictures of that godforsaken wedding instead of the bonuses my workers earned. You should have seen the looks on their faces last night. I'll never forget it as long as I live. I'll never feel good about myself again . . ."

"Dad, take it easy."

"Richard, everyone's calling me for interviews. Everyone's calling me cheap. I'm ashamed to walk around the store today. My oldest customers are disgusted with me, I can tell. Not to mention that without my key people, this place is falling apart. And we're catering the Festival . . ."

"I don't have to be in New York until Monday. I'll jump in the car and ride on up. I worked often enough at the store to know what I'm doing."

"Richard, I hate to make you do that. Your play just ended and you have a few days off."

"Forget it, Dad. I'll see you in a couple of hours."

Sam was choked up. It would be so nice to see a friendly face. "Thank you, son," he said. "You don't know what this means to me."

Feeling somewhat better, Sam hung up the phone. I'll have a cup of coffee, he thought, then get back out there to face the firing squad. He walked over to the coffeepot he always kept in his office. He was reaching for his mug when the door burst open. Without turning, he knew who it was. Everyone else in the store would have knocked before coming in. Everyone but his bride of six months. Sam braced himself.

"I just fired that kid in produce!" Rhoda snapped. "He's useless!"

Sam spun around. "You fired him! When we need all the help we can get, you fired him! Ten to one he's outside giving an interview right now."

"He was rude to me when I tried to show him how to stack tomatoes. Then he actually said it was no wonder everyone calls me The Skunk!"

Sam blinked. "The Skunk?"

"*The Skunk*. Behind my back, that's what they call me."

That's pretty good Sam thought as he stared at the white stripe in Rhoda's jet black hair. He was amused and embarrassed at the same time. The folks around here have her number, and they must think I'm an idiot for marrying her. "You had no right to fire that boy," he said angrily. "Zach tries hard and he's a good kid. I'm going to go out and try and catch him."

"And go against my wishes?" Rhoda asked, appalled. "With all I'm doing to keep this place going today?"

Sam pointed his finger at her. "I can tell you one thing right now. I wouldn't have even *needed* your help around here if you hadn't tortured me into giving those stupid pictures to my five key workers. We were like family until you came along. Millionaires or not, they would have been here first thing this morning to help us get through the Festival, and we would have had ourselves a blast!"

"How *dare* you?" Rhoda asked, her eyes blazing.

"How dare *you?*"

"I'm packing my bags and heading to Boston for the weekend. Thank God my apartment hasn't sold yet." She rushed past him, hurrying back into the store. "Enjoy the Festival!" she screamed over her shoulder.

"I will now!" he called after her, as customers stopped pushing their carts to hear the exchange. "And do me a favor," he added, unable to contain himself, "take your la-dee-dah apartment off the market!"

As one, the customers burst into applause.

# 18

That's where he was all night! On the basement floor, listening to crooks make fun of him and all the other people they swindled!" Alvirah exclaimed, as she, Regan, Jack, and Glenda drove to Duncan's house.

"Yes!" Glenda answered.

"I'm sure glad he got his hands on their ticket. You mean to say that he gave it to you to hold?"

"He didn't know what else to do. I think he's in shock."

"Must be," Alvirah murmured. "Can I see it?"

"Sure. I'm scared to death to be carrying this ticket. I keep feeling in my pocket to make sure it's still there." Glenda pulled it out. "Here it is."

Reverently, Alvirah took the ticket, studied it, shook her head, and leaned forward. "Have a look for yourself, Regan. I doubt if you'll hold anything worth that much again."

Jack had been listening intently. "You know, Glenda," he began, "Duncan may not want those crooks to get the money. But we're going to have to hand the ticket over to the police. I can assure you that if those guys have been swindling people, there won't be any payment to them until all their victims have been compensated."

"Duncan would hate to see them collect on this ticket, but what he's most concerned about is having them locked up." Glenda paused. "Could Duncan be in trouble for taking the ticket?" she asked anxiously. "Would it be considered stolen property?"

"That's the last thing I'd worry about. I doubt those two will be in any position to press charges against him."

The farther they drove out of town, the more rural the landscape became. The houses were farther apart, and it seemed as though all of them had Christmas decorations. One farmhouse had a real sleigh with a life-sized Santa on the roof.

"We're getting close," Glenda noted. "It's this next street up here on the right. The road curves a little, and Duncan's house is the last one at the end of the lane."

A moment later, she murmured, "Oh, look, there's someone parked in front."

As they approached, a van with the BUZ logo began to move and drove past them.

"They're doing the 'before' shots for the lifestyles of the rich and famous," Alvirah commented.

"Wait till they see *my* house," Glenda said as Jack pulled into Duncan's driveway. "I'll get the keys out of Duncan's ignition. I put them back this morning. I didn't know what else to do with them."

When they entered the house, they heard the phone ringing. "I may as well answer it," Glenda said and hurried to pick it up. "Hello."

"Hello," a woman chirped. "Is Mr. Duncan Graham there?"

"No, he's not. Would you like to leave a message?"

"Yes indeed. We're raising money for People Against Government in Any Way, Shape, or Form. We'd like to schedule a meeting with him to get his input into . . ."

Glenda dropped the phone back into the cradle. "A crazy who wants to relieve Duncan of his money before he even collects it," she said.

"Brace yourself," Alvirah advised. "You're all going to be hearing from a lot of them. People say they come out of the woodwork. I say they come from Mars."

Glenda pointed to the stacks of papers on the small dining room table. "Regan, those are the notes on the financial course I told you about."

"Let's take a quick look and see if there's any paperwork on the oil well investment."

They divided the pages and flipped through them.

"They sound like geniuses," Alvirah said, holding up one page. "Turn off the lights when you leave a room. Decide what you want before you open the refrigerator door. Holding it open wastes money." She put the paper down. "You mean to tell me Duncan *paid* for this kind of advice?"

"I never know what I want to eat until I've looked inside the refrigerator to see what appeals to me," Jack said.

"I don't think there's anything here about an oil well," Alvirah grumbled. "Unless it was written in disappearing ink."

"There's nothing here," Regan confirmed. "But they must have given him some kind of receipt for his five thousand dollars."

"Unless we find some proof of a scam, our hands are tied," Jack said.

"I don't think Duncan would mind if I took a quick look around," Glenda said. "He asked me to help him with this."

"I know you think I'm kidding, but check under his mattress," Alvirah suggested.

"You *are* kidding," Glenda said. "Or are you?"

"I'm not. I had five different cleaning jobs every week. At two of them people kept money and important papers under the mattress. One of the others thought it was a good hiding spot for her diary. I'm proud to say I never read a word of it." Alvirah paused. "Not that I wasn't tempted. That lady was something else."

Glenda headed for the bedroom. A moment later, her voice triumphant, she called, "Alvirah! I can't believe it! You were right!" She came rushing back into the living room, opening a legal-sized envelope with the logo of a gushing oil well, and handed it to Jack.

"Oh, boy," Jack muttered. "Those guys are shameless. Let's see what's inside." He extricated a document from the envelope, holding it carefully by the edge. "This may be valuable for fingerprints," he explained as the others read it with him.

"They sure tried to make this look official, but I can tell you right now that seal is a joke." Alvirah sighed. "Some of the people in my support groups who were scammed had documents that looked just like this one."

"I'll call my office and have them run a check on this company," Jack said. "As soon as they verify it's not legit, we'll contact the district attorney's office. They'll obtain warrants to arrest those crooks."

"Poor Duncan," Glenda said. "He worked hard for every penny he turned over to those jerks, and all he ends up with is this Mickey Mouse certificate. It's so sad."

"Twelve million bucks should cheer him up, Glenda," Jack said with a half smile as he reached for his cell phone.

Regan turned to Glenda. "Duncan shouldn't stay here tonight. For that matter, you shouldn't be alone in your house either."

"With Harvey running around town, I don't want to be," Glenda said emphatically. "I'll pack a bag for Duncan. We'd both be better off staying at the Inn with all of you."

"Good idea. Now, where did he say to look for his cell phone?"

"It's probably somewhere around the easy chair."

"I'll look." Alvirah walked over to the chair. "Not on the seat, not on the armrest . . . here it is, it had started to slip down the side . . ." She had no sooner picked up the phone than it began to ring. She looked at the caller ID. "It says 'Mom and Dad.' Isn't that sweet?"

"Let me have it," Glenda said. "Duncan left a message for his parents when he was waiting for the ambulance." She raised the phone to her ear. "Hello, this is Duncan's friend Glenda," she began then waited. "He's fine, Mrs. Graham, don't worry. Yes, he *has* won twelve million dollars. . . . you slept late? . . . uh huh. . . . I don't think you need to charter a plane to be with him. . . . He's at the hospital getting his leg checked out. . . . I'm bringing his cell phone to him, and I'll make sure he calls you. Bye."

She slipped the phone in her purse. "Duncan's parents are what you call night owls. They just woke up. The first they heard of all this was the message Duncan left for them."

"They must have clear consciences," Alvirah said.

"That's for sure," Regan agreed. "But they were spared a lot of worry."

While Glenda was packing for Duncan, Alvirah and Regan studied the framed pictures on the mantel. One of them was of a young woman with shoulder-length light brown hair. "This must be Flower," Regan said. "If Duncan's going to stay at the Inn, I bet he'd be glad to have her photo with him."

Fifteen minutes later they were driving down a crowded Main Street, heading toward the hospital.

"It's only a few hours until the Festival begins," Glenda said. "What's that up ahead? Oh, I don't believe it!"

A reporter, with a cameraman behind him, was talking to a crowd gathered in front of the window of Pettie's jewelry store. "They must all be gawking at Duncan's ring. Let's stop for a minute," Glenda said heatedly. "Regan, that was a good idea you had for me to tell the others I was picking up the ring as an excuse for leaving the luncheon. And that's just what I'm going to do. Jack, there's a parking spot over there. Could you grab it?"

"Sure."

"Do you think the jeweler will let you have the ring?" Regan asked. "He's getting a lot of publicity, which is exactly what he wants."

"He'd better."

"We'll go in with you," Jack volunteered. "We'll make sure he hands it over." He parked the car, and they all got out.

As they passed the reporter, they heard him ask, "I want all of you who think Duncan Graham should spring for a better ring for his girlfriend to raise your hands."

Glenda shot the reporter a look of contempt as she, Jack, and Regan hurried into the jewelry store. Before following them, Alvirah glanced into the display window, then stopped dead in her tracks. With a murmured apology, she maneuvered her way through the crowd to get a better look. Her eyes widened as she stared at the ring with its center diamond surrounded by petal-like semiprecious stones. Then she opened the top buttons of her coat, reached inside, and flicked on the hidden microphone of the sunburst pin that she had fastened to her lapel that morning. Whenever she was on a case and interviewing a person of interest, she always backed up her memory with recorded conversations.

As Alvirah entered the store, the jeweler was reaching into the display window for the ring, a disgruntled look on his face. He grew even more disgruntled as the crowd roared in protest.

"He's not happy, but he agreed to let us have the ring," Regan told Alvirah.

"What's more important is where he got it," Alvirah whispered. "Unless I've lost my mind, which I haven't, this ring was missing after Kitty Whelan, the best friend of Mrs. O'Keefe, my Friday cleaning job, was found dead on the floor."

# 19

Betty, what are you doing?" Edmund asked desperately. "Are you crazy?"

"Not too crazy to know that this girl has ears," she said angrily as she easily held a struggling Flower in her powerful arms. She looked down. "Flower, meet your boyfriend's financial advisers. They're real geniuses."

"What are you talking about?" Woodrow asked.

"Her boyfriend won the lottery last night."

"Which one is her boyfriend?"

"Duncan."

"Duncan!" both men cried at once.

"Yes. Lucky for him he didn't listen to your advice."

"He *did* follow our advice," Edmund said. "He didn't play, but his friends are cutting him in."

"We didn't follow our own advice," Woodrow said. "We bought the other winning ticket, but we think Duncan stole it from us."

"What? How did you manage that?" Betty asked derisively.

Sputtering, Edmund began to explain. "Someone was in our house last night. We heard a sound like something falling on the basement stairs, and like fools we didn't investigate. But whoever was down there would have heard us talking and knew we hid our ticket in the freezer. We're pretty sure it was Duncan."

"Why?"

"We heard on the radio that he was missing all night, then he showed up an hour ago, hobbling as though he took a spill somewhere." Edmund paused then added, "And we did use the numbers he told us he was planning to play."

Terrified as she was, Flower felt a wave of pure joy go through her. She was sure Duncan hadn't abandoned her after all. How could I ever have lost faith in my Duncan Donuts? she wondered.

"This makes it all easy," Woodrow said. "Duncan gives us our ticket, we give him back his girlfriend."

"He dumped her," Betty hissed. "He hasn't called her since he won. He might not be so willing . . ."

Flower, her faith restored in Duncan, tried to bite Betty's hand.

"Down, girl," Betty said, "or I'll turn you back into a pile of mush." She looked at the cousins. "If you do get that ticket, you're going to split the money four ways with me and Jed."

"That's a little excessive, Betty," Edmund moaned.

"Excessive? Jed and I can't stay here now and neither can

we stand around here with her all day," she said impatiently. "We've got a full house. Some of the others will be back for tea."

"I'm sure they will," Woodrow said sarcastically. "Your scones are delicious."

Betty looked as if she wanted to kill him. "Grab one of those dish towels. There's twine over there in the drawer by the stove . . ."

What are they going to do to me? Flower wondered. Especially Betty. She's evil. Flower felt Betty's hand loosen its grip, but before she could even try to scream, Woodrow stuffed a dish towel in her mouth and tied it tightly. Edmund twisted twine around her feet. Betty yanked her arms behind her and held them for Edmund to secure.

"Let's bring her back to the shed," Betty ordered. "Woodrow, grab the tablecloth in that chest by the hearth. We'll cover her with it."

Woodrow did as he was told. "I'll carry her," he offered, the cloth in his hand.

"No, you've done enough damage by showing up here today. You'll probably drop her on her head." Betty threw Flower over her shoulder with one quick motion and waited impatiently as Woodrow fumbled to shake open the cloth and wrap it around their captive. "Jed's going to have a fit when he sees this," Betty grumbled. "Come on."

Flower's instinct was to kick, but she knew it was useless. She felt a blast of cold air as she was rushed from the house.

Edmund ran ahead and opened the door to the shed. Once inside, Betty dropped Flower down on an old lawn chair and roughly pulled off the tablecloth. Her eyes adjusting to the light, Flower took in the gloomy surroundings. A work bench was cluttered with rusty paint cans; shovels and rakes hung haphazardly from the walls; a snow blower with a flat tire was just inches from her legs. She gasped as a section of the back wall slid open and Jed, the kindly proprietor who had carried her bags, appeared. Behind him, Flower could see a large computer screen and an orderly work space with high-tech equipment.

Looking furious, Jed barked, "I knew it would be trouble for us when you two came to town!"

"This is thanks to your wife's rudeness," Edmund shouted, his voice agitated and trembling. "If she had just been polite and let us in . . ."

"Jed, get out of the way," Betty ordered. "We've got to keep her hidden in your office."

"What?" Jed protested. "Betty, we don't want her to see what's in there . . ."

"It doesn't matter now," Betty said. "We'll be on the run as long as this little Flower keeps blooming."

# 20

You broke the tibia bone near the ankle." Dr. Rusch, an older man with salt-and-pepper hair and rimless glasses, held up the X-rays as he spoke. "How did you manage that?"

"I fell down a flight of stairs," Duncan replied.

"Lucky you didn't do further damage by hobbling on that leg." He patted Duncan's arm. "You're going to be in a plaster cast for about six weeks." He smiled. "But I gather you don't have to worry about missing work."

"I guess not," Duncan said weakly.

"Does it feel pretty sore now?"

"Kind of," Duncan admitted.

"I'm going to give you something to dull the pain. It might make you a little drowsy."

"Doctor, I don't have my cell phone. I hate to ask, but would you mind lending me yours? I need to talk to my girl-friend for a minute."

This is a first, Rusch thought with amusement. No pa-tient has ever asked to borrow my phone. I guess having boatloads of money does change one's mindset. "Duncan, I'm afraid you're not allowed to use a cell phone in here. How's this? Give me the number. I'll have the receptionist call and give her your message."

Trying not to sound too disappointed, Duncan said, "If she could just tell my girlfriend I'll call later. Thank you."

Ten minutes later the doctor came back to the cubicle in the emergency room . "She must be a popular lady. Her mailbox is full."

There's something wrong, Duncan thought. I *know* there's something wrong.

A nurse came up to his bedside. She handed him a tablet and a glass of water. "This will make you feel better. It's going to be a little while before we can take you in for the cast. We have a couple of skiers ahead of you. Why don't you just try and take a nap?"

Duncan swallowed the pill, leaned back, and closed his eyes. A sense of foreboding drove away his ability to relax and drift into sleep. Flower's voice kept running through his head. "I'm scared, Duncan," she was whispering. "Help me. I'm scared."

# 21

Horace Pettie threw the WE MISS YOU sign in the back of the store, then plopped the ring down on a velvet pad on the counter. "I held this for Duncan, on a fifty-dollar deposit, for six months," he said sourly. "I don't know any other jeweler who'd have done that. Displaying the ring in the window these last few hours has helped sell my Festival of Joy charms. Now Duncan gets all upset because people get a look at his ring? Too bad about him."

"That's right," Luella agreed quickly, as she tied a red bow on a gift-wrapped package and handed it to the only other customer now in the store. "I've worked for Mr. Pettie for twenty years. He's never been anything but the soul of kindness to the people of Branscombe. It just goes to show, no good deed goes unpunished. Isn't that right Mrs. Graney?"

The spry septuagenarian nodded. "Mmmm hmmmm. It seems to me that Duncan Graham doesn't have to care about anybody now that he has twelve million dollars. Merry Christmas everyone," she trilled as she left the store.

Alvirah watched the door close behind her. "Now we can talk. Excuse me, sir, but I need to know where you got that ring."

Horace Pettie looked startled. "Why are you asking?"

"Because it was probably stolen," Alvirah said, checking again to be sure the microphone in her sunburst pin was on.

Pettie's lips tightened. "If you're implying I obtained this ring in some underhanded way, you're mighty wrong, and I'd appreciate you leaving my store this minute."

"I'm not accusing you of anything, and I certainly don't mean to upset you," Alvirah replied hastily. "But I can tell you that ring disappeared from the home of a woman who died under suspicious circumstances eight years ago in New York City."

"What?" Glenda asked, her eyes widening.

Jack pointed to it. "This ring, Alvirah?"

Alvirah nodded. "That ring. I'm sure of it."

The bracelets on Luella's right arm jangled as she slapped her hand on the counter. "How can you be so sure it's the same ring?" she asked angrily.

"The lady who owned it, Kitty Whelan, loved to garden. Her husband had the ring made for her for their fiftieth anniversary with the diamond in the center and the petals the color of her favorite flowers." Alvirah pointed. "Look— white for lilies, red for roses, yellow for daffodils, and purple for pansies. Kitty just *loved* that ring. After her husband died she wore it every day. I worked for a woman named Bridget O'Keefe who was a good friend of Kitty's. I was only there on Fridays, but before Kitty had a heart attack, she often dropped by. I saw this ring many times. Kitty always boasted that it was one of a kind, made only for her. But when Kitty's nephew found her dead at the foot of her staircase, she didn't have the ring on. He never found it when he cleared out the house."

"Maybe she had a special hiding place for the ring when she wasn't wearing it," Luella said. "You know how many times we've heard about jewelry that has turned up in the most unlikely places? After years and years?"

"You're right about that," Alvirah agreed. "But there's more to this story. Kitty's nephew discovered that her savings account had been almost cleaned out, most likely by a companion who had worked for Kitty the last few months before she died. This of course raised the question if the fall down the stairs that killed her was accidental. But by this time the companion had disappeared into thin air, never to be seen again."

"Those stories disgust me." Luella sighed. "A lady in my sister's town was robbed blind by a so-called"—she paused and held up her fingers, making invisible quotation marks midair—" 'helper.' Turns out the 'helper' was doing all the food shopping for her own family and friends and charging it to the old lady's credit card. Thousands of dollars spent on food, and the woman weighed ninety pounds! Why the accountant didn't call it to somebody's attention is beyond me. It took a suspicious cashier who knew the dear old soul had not only gone into the hospital, but was also allergic to seafood, to raise a red flag. When the 'helper' tried to charge fifteen lobsters and three cases of beer, the cashier reported it to his boss. Turns out it was the 'helper's' boyfriend's birthday. She was throwing a party for him and his thuggish friends." Luella dropped her hands. "It was a disgrace."

I just wasted precious tape on that story, Alvirah thought. "So you understand what I'm talking about?"

"*I* do," Pettie said. Obviously relieved he was not being accused of wrongdoing, he was enjoying the drama surrounding Duncan's ring. "I understand completely. As a matter of fact, I've got a story about my wife's cousin who . . ." The door opened, and new customers walked in. Pettie quickly cut himself off. "But I won't bore you with that now," he said hurriedly. "To answer your question, this ring was found on the street by a man who's lived in Branscombe all his life. His name is Rufus Blackstone. He left it with me on consignment, and, let me tell you, he wasn't as nice as I was about letting Duncan put it on hold for so long. He's a crusty old codger. I'll go in the back and look up his number for you. Glenda, you said you're paying for this on your credit card?"

"Let me pay for it," Alvirah said. "The ring should go

back to Kitty's nephew. And Kitty had said she wanted Mrs. O'Keefe to have it if she died first. She was adamant about that."

"Poor Duncan," Glenda said. "I'm sure he wouldn't want it now, but he told me he thought this ring would be perfect for his girlfriend because her name is Flower."

"If he wants, I can make him a copy with real stones," Pettie volunteered, his face brightening. "It will be *gorgeous*!"

"We'll pass that on to him," Glenda said wryly.

Pettie hurried away with Alvirah's credit card. Luella was just beginning her sales pitch to three giggling young girls wearing Branscombe High School cheerleader jackets. "You all should have one of these charms. You'll love it! And what better way to always remember the Festival of Joy?"

Jack turned to Regan and mumbled. "I don't think we'll need a charm to remember this Festival."

"I don't think so," Regan agreed. "Alvirah, did you ever meet Kitty's companion?"

"Just once for a minute. She and Kitty were getting out of a cab when I was leaving. I wish I'd taken a better look at her, but I was carrying out two big bags of garbage. Mrs. O'Keefe seemed to manufacture pounds of junk on a weekly basis."

Pettie reappeared with a small gift bag, an index card, and a receipt for Alvirah. "Could I get your John Hancock on this, Mrs. Meehan?" he asked.

"Sure."

"And here's Rufus Blackstone's number. I just rang him up, but he's not home and he doesn't have an answering machine. I thought it would be a good idea to let him know that you'd be calling and also to give him the good news that he can pick up a check from me. If I get a chance, I'll try him again."

"Thanks," Alvirah said. "We'll catch up with him later. I just have to find out where this ring has been for the last eight years."

"Wait till Duncan hears this," Glenda said as they started out the door.

"Don't forget to tell him I can make up a beautiful ring for him in no time flat!" Pettie called after them.

The crowd outside the window had dispersed.

# 22

After making sure that Flower was securely tied, gagged, and immobilized, Betty, Jed, Woodrow, and Edmund left Jed's secret office and went back into the house.

Woodrow walked to the stove where the freshly baked cake was sitting on the rack. He broke a piece off and crammed it in his mouth. "Not bad," he pronounced.

Betty grabbed the baking pan. "Keep your mitts off my cake!" she snapped.

"The only thing I've had to eat today was a couple of pieces of candy," Woodrow complained. "We were on our way to a nice lunch in Boston when we found out we were victims of a terrible crime."

"Jed, fix them something to eat," Betty ordered. "Then you two have to stay out of sight. People are going to be coming here soon for tea. I'll get Flower's gear out of her room now."

"Out of sight? Where should we go?" Edmund asked. "Don't say the shed. It's cold."

"There's only one place you *can* go. The basement. I can't have you sitting here if somebody comes through that swinging door."

"The basement?" Woodrow complained. "You've got to be kidding."

"You're not exactly honored guests," Betty snapped. "I'll be right back."

At the reception desk she reached in the drawer for Flower's credit card receipt and tore it into shreds. Thank God Jed hadn't validated the card yet, she thought. Then a terrible thought occurred to Betty. Had Flower spoken to anyone since she checked in?

Betty hurried upstairs to Flower's room. A cell phone was on the bed. Betty turned it on, held her breath, and pressed "dialed calls." The last call Flower had made was early this morning. Betty exhaled slowly then pressed "received calls." There hadn't been any today, which meant that Flower hadn't answered the phone after she checked in. Betty could see there were messages but would need Flower's passcode to listen to them. If I want it, she'll give it to me, Betty thought darkly, as she turned off the phone and dropped it in the pocket of her apron.

It was clear that Flower hadn't gotten under the bed covers. Betty smoothed the spread and fluffed up the pillows. In the bathroom, she tossed Flower's toiletries into her knapsack, wiped out the sink with a towel, and walked back into the bedroom. She took a quick look around for anything she might have missed, then grabbed Flower's coat from the chair.

In the hallway, she tossed the towel down the laundry chute and momentarily stuffed Flower's things in the linen closet. To be certain that no one had returned while they were in the shed, Betty knocked on, then opened the doors of the other five guest rooms with the master key. Satisfied that the second floor was empty, she retrieved the knapsack and coat, hurried down the stairs, and locked the front door. Now anyone who shows up will be forced to ring the bell, she thought. I can't take a chance on someone else having big ears like Flower.

In the kitchen, Edmund and Woodrow were slurping vegetable soup. Flower's nearly full bowl was still on the table. I should have told her we don't serve lunch, Betty thought angrily. This is what I get for being too nice.

She sat down at the seat Flower had never excused herself from, threw Flower's coat on a chair, and started rummaging through her knapsack. "Nothing," she said dismissively. Then, from a zippered compartment, she fished out Flower's wallet. When she opened it, the first thing she saw was a picture of Flower and Duncan, their heads close together, smiling blissfully. She held it up. "Get a load of this."

"Romeo and Juliet," Woodrow grunted as he scraped the bottom of the soup bowl with his spoon.

"What a pair. They both ended up dead," Edmund commented.

"We all know how it ended, Edmund," Woodrow said impatiently. "You always like to act as though you're smarter than me."

"No need for acting," Edmund shot back. "You're the one who wanted to leave the ticket in the freezer. At least I knew that was a stupid idea. If we had taken the ticket, we'd be having a big juicy steak in Boston right now."

"Stop it!" Jed growled savagely. "There's no way this is going to end well for me and Betty! We want out!"

There was a moment of silence in the kitchen as the impact of what he was saying sank in on the Winthrop cousins.

"I like our life here in Branscombe," Jed continued heatedly. "I don't want to leave." He turned to Betty. "Do you?"

"Not really." Betty agreed. "Traveling is very stressful these days, never mind being on the run. Jed hasn't been feeling that well. He likes to stay home at night watching television. We've turned into homebodies. And it's not so bad. Whatever it takes, no more running."

Jed nodded. "If we get involved with kidnapping, and we hold that little girl for ransom, there's no way we can stay here. Betty and I like Branscombe, and we like New Hampshire. We like the snow, and Betty has turned into a good little baker, as you may have noticed."

"Listen to them," Woodrow said to Edmund. "You'd think they were Ma and Pa Kettle." He turned to Jed. "What about the fact that you're cheating people with your Internet schemes and stealing from your guests' homes months after their wonderful stay at The Hideaway?"

"That's just to keep me busy! It might not be right, but it's small potatoes compared to kidnapping charges. And even if you did get your lottery ticket back in exchange for that girl, there's no guarantee you'll end up with any money. The day someone tries to collect on that ticket, the lottery office will be swarming with Feds. And Lord knows we can't trust you two to pay me and Betty our share if you somehow *did* collect. Why, you didn't even call us to give us the good news that you'd won, now did you?"

"We were going to . . ." Woodrow said.

"Honestly, we were," Edmund said. "We were just so excited . . ."

"Oh, sure. Let me tell you something. If we let that girl go, ten minutes later every cop in New Hampshire will be hunting us down."

"What are you suggesting?"

"I'm suggesting that if you want to get your ticket back from Duncan, don't say one word to him about the girl. Threaten him about his own safety if you have to. He's getting that other lottery money. Maybe he'll give you back your ticket. But I'm warning you, don't make any deals to exchange Flower for the ticket." Jed glared coldly at the cousins.

"Then what do we do with her?" Edmund asked. "We can't just leave her back there."

"Of course we can't! You think *we* want her around?" Jed exclaimed. "There's only one solution." He lowered his voice. "When it gets dark, we'll put her in the trunk of your car and drive up to the lake at Devil's Pass. We'll weight her down with a block of cement. That lake is big and cold and deep. She'll never be seen again."

Edmund and Woodrow stared at him in shock. "Kidnapping offends you, but murder doesn't?" Edmund asked, his voice barely audible.

Jed shrugged.

"I see," Edmund mumbled weakly.

"Going to prison again is what offends me," Jed said vehemently. "There's a lot better chance we'll get caught if we hold her for ransom. This way she'll disappear without a trace."

"Let me try and trade Flower for the lottery ticket," Woodrow begged. "We promise we'll pay you as soon as we get the money. Just think of all the nice places in the world you can visit . . ."

"We've made our choice," Betty said with finality. "No more running."

Jed looked out the window. "At 5:00 it'll be dark and the whole town will be gathering at that candlelight ceremony. We'll make our move then and get it over with. After that,

Betty and I would appreciate it if you two made yourself scarce. We don't want any more trouble."

"Make ourselves scarce?" Edmund gasped. "We have no place to go and we can't leave Branscombe without that ticket. Your basement actually sounds very nice. Can't we stay there just for tonight?"

# 23

The celebratory luncheon at the Branscombe Inn was winding up.

Tommy's parents were sitting on either side of him, their attitude fiercely protective, as if a wanton woman might appear at any moment out of nowhere and ensnare their newly wealthy son. "I know Tommy would like to meet the right girl, but now it's going to be even harder," his mother, Ruth, said. "She's going to have to pass the test with us, and believe me, we'll put her through the ringer, right, Burt?" she asked her husband.

As usual, when his wife wanted him to agree, Burt's head nodded affirmatively. "Tommy's a good boy," he declared. "He's always deserved the best, even when he didn't have a dime in his pocket. When you see how someone as smart as Sam Conklin can get swept off his feet and rush into a disaster, it scares you. To think Sam was married all those years to Maybelle, one of the sweetest, nicest ladies who ever walked the face of the earth, and then he marries a woman nobody knows." Burt looked around the table. "What do you all call her, the Raccoon?"

"The Skunk, Dad," Tommy corrected him, increasingly embarrassed by the drift of the conversation. "Don't worry about me, I'll be fine. Believe me."

"That skunk!" Ralph's wife, Judy, cried. "Boy was she guilty of bad timing. I hear things are a mess over at Conklin's right now, and I couldn't be happier!"

"You have?" Muffy asked anxiously. "I hope there won't be any problem with the food for the Festival."

"Don't worry, Muffy," Ralph said with a wave of his hand. "We did so much advance preparation that they should be able to handle it without us."

"I hope so. This is Branscombe's first Festival of Joy, and we want to make a good impression on all our visitors plus everyone who tunes in to the special."

Marion pushed back her chair. "Festival or no Festival, we've got to get to the bank. I won't rest easy until we put that lottery ticket in a safe deposit box and see them lock the vault." She turned to Nora. "I've just loved chatting with you. Hope to see you later."

"We'll all see each other later," Muffy said enthusiastically. "Everyone in town is going to be at the opening of the Festival. I hope Duncan can be there. It's wonderful that he made it back safely from wherever he was. It would have been such a downer if he were still missing."

That's one way of putting it, Luke thought. Since Willy

came into the room without Alvirah, he knew that Nora was chomping at the bit to find out the real reason Alvirah had gone with Regan and Jack. She obviously didn't buy the story that Alvirah was dying to get a look at Branscombe. Luke didn't either.

"Oh Duncan's back, all right," Tommy's mother said to Muffy, a hint of derision in her voice. "And I notice he didn't turn down the chance to be included in the winning group."

"Mom," Tommy said hurriedly. "Remember the number 32. That was Duncan's Powerball number. We wouldn't be sitting here now if he hadn't chosen it."

"I suppose," she acquiesced. "We'll go to the bank with you, son."

Muffy turned to Nora. "I would just love to drive you around our pretty little town this afternoon. We can stop by the church bazaar where we'll get a sneak preview of all the wonderful things that will be on sale starting tonight. They'll be putting the final touches on everything, and I can show you where you'll be doing the story hour tomorrow. Does that sound good?" As was her custom, she answered herself. "I think it sounds great! I just wish Regan were here. Maybe she can catch up with us later. Willy, Luke—does a tour of our village sound agreeable to you?"

"Yes," they both answered quickly, if only to stop the flow of talk.

"Muffy," Nora said, "Luke and Willy and I haven't even

been to our rooms yet. Why don't we meet you in the lobby in twenty minutes?"

"Super!"

The Reillys and Meehans had rooms across the hall from each other on the second floor. As they were getting off the elevator, Nora said, "Willy, could you come into our room for a minute?" It wasn't a question.

Here we go, Luke thought. "Get ready for the interrogation, Willy," he warned.

Willy rolled his eyes. "Regan swore me to secrecy."

"She didn't mean us," Nora assured him.

"Yes, she did," Luke said positively.

"Oh, Luke, stop it," Nora said, laughing, "hurry up and open the door." They were barely inside the room when she spun around. "Willy, what's going on? What made Alvirah take off with them?"

Even Luke's usually unflappable demeanor registered shock and disbelief as Willy filled them in. "You mean to tell me they're riding around with a lottery ticket worth 180 million dollars that belongs to two criminals?" he asked.

"That about sums it up," Willy answered, as he reached for the door handle. "I'd better go powder my nose. I'll see you downstairs in fifteen minutes."

# 24

The sixtyish receptionist in the emergency room of Branscombe General Hospital looked up when the group appeared at her desk. Spotting Glenda, she smiled. "I saw you on TV. You're one of the lottery winners!"

"Yes, I am," Glenda replied. "Trust me. I still can't believe it. We're here to see my fellow winner, Duncan Graham."

"I just tried to call his girlfriend for him, but her message box was full. What a lucky girl she is! As my grandmother would say, she certainly landed in a tub of butter."

"My mother used that expression, too," Alvirah said, thinking that her mother's version was a little more colorful.

"Granny had a saying for everything," the receptionist said with a laugh. She pointed to a door. "He's right through there. The third cubicle on the right. I shouldn't let you all in at once, but we don't have any serious cases at the moment. Just a bunch of broken bones."

"Is that all?" Jack muttered as they went through the door.

They reached the third curtained cubicle. "Duncan?" Glenda called.

"I'm here," Duncan replied, his voice faint.

Glenda pulled back the curtain.

Alvirah took in the sight of the unshaven, pale, anxious-looking figure on the bed. He doesn't look like he could use any more bad news, she thought.

"Glenda!" Duncan said, trying to sit up. "Do you have my cell phone?"

"Right here." Quickly she handed it to him. "I think you've met Jack Reilly." She began to introduce him to Regan and Alvirah, but Duncan interrupted.

"I'm sorry to be rude but I'm worried about my girl-friend. Maybe she was in an accident . . ." He checked his messages. "She still hasn't called me!"

A nurse approached. "Mr. Graham, it's time to take you in for your cast. And you must turn off that phone. They're not permitted in here." She turned to the others. "This won't take long. You can wait outside."

"Glenda," Duncan said quickly. "Would you please try to reach Flower? Her number must still be on your phone. If you can't reach her, please call her work number. That must be on your phone, too—I called earlier. Ask if they know where she is." His eyes were sick with worry.

"Of course, Duncan. I'll make the calls, and we'll be wait-ing for you outside." She turned to the nurse. "Will he be able to leave as soon as his cast is on?"

"Absolutely. We'll fit him with crutches, and off he goes."

The four of them retreated to the waiting room. Glenda tried Flower's phone, but her mailbox was still full. She then tried Flower's work number. A woman with a soothing voice answered. "Precious Darlings Day Care."

Not all of them, I'm sure, Glenda thought. "Hello, may I speak to the manager?"

"We're fully enrolled for the next four years," the woman said proudly.

"No, I'm not calling about that," Glenda said. "It's very important I speak to someone about one of the employees. Flower . . ." Glenda realized she didn't know Flower's last name. But how many Flowers could be working there?

"Oh, yes, Flower," the woman said.

"I'm calling for her boyfriend who just broke his leg, and he really wants to reach her."

"Duncan broke his leg?"

"Yes. Do you know him?"

"No. But Flower talks about him all the time. He called earlier."

"Yes, he did. He's concerned that he hasn't been able to reach her and didn't know that she was taking today off."

"Wait a minute. It's mid-afternoon there, right?"

"Yes."

"Oh, dear."

Glenda's heart sank. "What do you mean?"

"Flower was flying in to surprise him today. She took the

red-eye to Boston last night, then was planning to take an early morning bus to where Duncan lives. She should have been there *hours* ago. And it's odd she isn't answering her phone."

"Do you by any chance know what flight she took?"

"I'm sorry, I don't."

"Okay," Glenda said. "If you hear from her, could you please call me or Duncan?" She recited their numbers.

"And if you hear anything, please call us," the woman said. "We love Flower. We were already feeling terrible that we might lose her soon."

# 25

The *Skunk*!" Rhoda thought as she turned the key in the lock of the three-bedroom home Sam had lived in since his marriage to Maybelle fifty years ago. She slammed the door so hard that several of Maybelle's figurines jiggled on the shelf over the foyer table. Too bad they didn't fall off, Rhoda thought. Sam had reluctantly agreed to allow her to redecorate but had insisted on keeping Maybelle's trinkets in place, which annoyed Rhoda no end. The living room of the colonial house had been done over with black leather couches and chairs, a white shag rug, and modern art that Sam complained he couldn't make head nor tail of. Paintings of mountains and lakes and flowers and animals had been relegated to the attic.

Maybelle's maple dining room furniture, with its corner cupboards and cushioned chairs, had been replaced by a glass table with massive steel legs and chairs shaped like triangles. Upstairs, Richard's boyhood room was now serving as Rhoda's office, and the former guest bedroom was filled with her exercise equipment.

Go back to my lah-dee-dah apartment, she thought, as she yanked off her coat and threw it over the bannister. I can't *wait* to pack up and get out of here! I'll fix his wagon! All I've tried to do for him, and he just takes me for granted. Through the window, she could see that the snow, which had been light and intermittent, was suddenly coming down harder. Oh no, she thought, I can't drive in this. By the time I get my things together, the roads will be slick, and I'll end up getting stuck in all that traffic going into Boston on a Friday night at holiday time. Good riddance to this burg—but not till tomorrow.

I took a shot at the country life, but it's not for me. Rhoda thought of her previous husbands, two of whom she had not mentioned to Samuel. It's not bad to be divorced twice, but *four* times suggests I can't get along with anyone and scares off potential suitors.

Samuel had seemed so easygoing, but she soon found out that he was stubborn as a mule. Getting him to agree to put his employees' bonus money in our retirement fund had been a struggle. I was only looking out for our future, she thought. Oh well, the prenup gives me $200,000 if we get divorced. I'll start off the New Year with that happy thought in mind. If I had known how much that geezer had in his savings account, I'd have insisted on more.

In the six months she'd lived in town, Rhoda had made

exactly one friend, Tishie Thornton, who never had anything nice to say about anyone and was the only human being in town Rhoda found who couldn't stand Maybelle. "From the time we were six years old, she was so annoyingly sweet," Tishie confided to a delighted Rhoda. "I have a beautiful singing voice, but *she* was the one always chosen for the solos in the school and then in the church choir. I couldn't bear the sight of her looking so innocent, holding her song book, singing with her eyes looking up to heaven like she was an angel. I finally quit the choir and never went back even after Maybelle died. I didn't want to hear all the talk about what a saint she was."

Rhoda stood for a moment in the quiet house. I don't want to hang around here all day, she thought. She hurried into the kitchen and picked up the phone. Tishie answered on the first ring.

"Rhoda, I hear you've had a rough day," Tishie said, trying not to sound pleased.

"You wouldn't believe it."

"No bonuses, huh?"

"They got paid well enough all year."

"I bet they did. And now look at them! They don't need your bonuses. Did you hear about the ring Duncan bought for his girlfriend?"

"I haven't heard anything. I was too busy picking apples off the floor."

"Duncan put a deposit on some kind of flowered ring at

Pettie's, and now he's bent out of shape. Turns out Pettie put the ring in the display window next to those Festival charms Luella's told me about at least a hundred times."

"A *flower* ring?" Rhoda repeated.

"Yes. A little diamond surrounded by colored stones shaped like petals."

"Who's his girlfriend?"

"Nobody knows. Who cares?"

"Who cares is right," Rhoda said, her mind flashing to the face of the young girl who was asking for Duncan this morning. "*I* certainly don't."

"So, what's up? I know you can't be calling just to chat what with everything going on at the store."

"Sam and I broke up. We're totally *kaput*. Finished. Bye-bye."

"So soon? I knew you'd be bored to tears by him. But you should have waited to get a Christmas present."

"He already bought it for me. A gorgeous bracelet we got in Boston when we went to see that son of his in a play. Sam almost had a heart attack when he signed the credit slip. The bracelet's in the safe, nicely gift wrapped. Don't worry, it's going with me."

"I'm proud of you, Rhoda. After all, you gave him the best six months of your life."

Rhoda laughed. "It *feels* like the best six years! Tishie, the weather's not great, so I'll have to put up with another night here. I was thinking, why don't we go to The Hideaway for tea this afternoon? That woman Betty is a little annoying with her saccharine sweetness . . ."

"Just like Maybelle was," Tishie interrupted.

"Don't remind me! I don't know if Betty can sing, but she sure knows how to bake. We can sit and gossip, away from all this hullabaloo about the Festival. I'm sick of it."

"Me, too. I can be there in half an hour, okay?"

"Tishie, I'm a city girl. I can't drive so well in the snow. Would you mind picking me up?"

"Not at all."

"Thanks, Tishie. If I hadn't met you, I probably would have been out of here months ago."

"Sorry about that. See you soon."

Rhoda hung up. Even though she could care less about Samuel, she felt a little let down. A sudden thought cheered her. There's got be a holiday singles dance for seniors somewhere in Boston tomorrow night. She'd gone to six of them in the month of December last year. She hadn't met anyone special, but who knows? There might be a new crop of widowers or divorcés that sprung up in the six months she'd been buried here. Maybe my next great romance will begin while Samuel is slaving over chicken potpie at the church supper. She began to hum as she ran upstairs to check her computer.

# 26

By the time Duncan was wheeled into the waiting room, his right leg in a cast from his knee to his ankle, Jack had learned from his office that Flower had been on a red-eye flight of Pacific Airlines that landed in Boston, where she had bought a bus ticket to Branscombe.

"But there hasn't been any further activity on the credit card she used to buy those tickets," Detective Joe Azzolino reported to his boss. "And that stock certificate is as phony as a three dollar bill."

As they had expected, Duncan's first question when he saw them was, "Have you reached Flower?"

"Not yet," Jack said. "Let's get you out to the car."

Alvirah's heart ached for Duncan as the attendant at the emergency room exit helped him up and handed him his crutches. At least I was able to walk out of the emergency room in New York on two feet, she thought, unconsciously patting the bandage over her eye.

Outside it had begun to snow hard. They were barely in

the car when Duncan asked anxiously, "Glenda, did you call the day care center?"

"Duncan, I'm sure everything's going to be all right . . ."

"What do you mean?" he demanded, his eyes suddenly frantic with worry.

"Flower took the day off. She flew to Boston on the red-eye last night and was planning to surprise you. We know she bought a bus ticket to Branscombe that would have gotten her here at about ten o'clock this morning."

"So where is she then? Why isn't she answering her phone?"

"We don't know, Duncan," Regan said quietly. "We thought we'd go down to the bus depot and make some inquiries to see if anyone remembers seeing her there. Glenda threw a few things in a bag for you because we think you should stay at the Inn tonight. We put a picture of a young woman you had on the mantel in it. We assumed it was Flower."

"Of course it's Flower! Who else would it be? Can I have it?" Duncan asked, his voice cracking.

Glenda retrieved the picture from the bag and gave it to him.

Duncan held it in his hands, his eyes suddenly moist. "Something's happened to her," he said, his voice trembling as he stared at the picture. "I'm sure of it. Even if she wanted to wait until tonight to surprise me, she'd be answering her phone. Those Winthrop thieves were on their way to Boston.

I told them about Flower when I talked to them about my goals in life. Could they have somehow run into her?"

"Did they ever see her picture?" Jack asked.

"No."

"Then it would seem unlikely, Duncan. But we did find out that the stock certificate is fraudulent. We'll have to go to the DA's office where you can swear out a complaint. They'll get an arrest warrant for those crooks."

"I don't care about that now! If they have Flower, it's a far worse crime than selling a phony oil well. Right now I don't care about an arrest warrant. We have to find Flower!"

"Absolutely," Jack agreed.

"I say we go to Conklin's first," Alvirah suggested. "If Flower arrived this morning and didn't know you were in on the lottery, she probably would have gone to see you at work. She doesn't have a key to your house, does she?"

"She's never been there," Duncan said sadly.

"She will be soon," Glenda encouraged. "Alvirah, I think that's a good idea to go directly to Conklin's, although I'm sure Mr. Conklin won't be too happy to see me after we dumped those miserable wedding pictures on his doorstep this morning. But I don't care what he thinks." She turned back to Duncan. "You'd better stay in the car. It's slippery, and all you need is another fall. I'll talk to everyone who's working today."

They reached the end of the hospital parking lot. "Which way, Glenda?" Jack asked.

"Turn right here and keep going."

When they pulled up in front of Conklin's, Regan turned to Glenda. "I'll come in with you. Duncan, how tall is Flower and how old is she?"

"She's twenty-four years old, but she looks younger. She's petite—about 5'3"."

"Can we have the picture, please?"

Reluctantly, Duncan handed it over.

Inside the store, Glenda heard a familiar voice. "Well, look who's here," Paige, a teenaged cashier called. "Don't tell me your ticket's a fake, and you want your job back?"

Glenda and Regan hurried over to Paige's register, where a woman pushing a cart filled with overflowing grocery bags had just been checked out. "Paige, I have to talk to you for a minute."

"Sure." Paige turned off the light at her station. "What's up, Moneybags?"

Glenda introduced her to Regan, held up Flower's picture, and explained the situation. ". . . she was on her way to visit Duncan and seems to be missing."

"Sounds like they make a good pair," Paige cracked as she snapped her gum. "Wasn't he missing overnight? I can't believe you guys cut him in on the lottery. You should have asked me. I would have thrown in a buck."

"Paige, I'm not kidding. This is serious."

"Oh, sorry."

"By any chance did you see this girl in the store today?"

Paige studied the picture. "No, I didn't see her. If she was here and bought anything, she didn't come through my register."

"Okay. We'll go around and speak to the others."

Paige lowered her voice. "Glenda, you missed the fireworks this morning. The Skunk had a shouting match with Mr. Conklin, and she stormed out. He told her to take her apartment in Boston off the market. Everyone here is so psyched! For us, the Festival of Joy is off and running."

"You're *kidding*!" Glenda exclaimed.

"Trust me, I'm not."

"It almost makes me want my job back."

"Oh, sure."

"Is Mr. Conklin in his office?"

"He's back in the kitchen with his sleeves rolled up. He even put on an apron. They have to get the trays of food ready and over to the Festival."

"That makes me feel guilty," Glenda murmured.

"It wouldn't make *me* feel guilty," Paige said, turning her light back on as a shopper approached. "It's his name over the door. Besides, I've never see him in a better mood."

Glenda and Regan showed Flower's picture to the other employees. They had all been there since early morning, and no one could remember seeing her.

"Regan, let's go talk to Mr. Conklin."

Regan followed her into the large kitchen where a half

dozen workers were rushing around, assembling platters of cold cuts and salads.

"Good work everyone!" Sam was saying. "We're getting that old teamwork spirit back in this store!" He turned and spotted Glenda. For a moment they looked at each other uncertainly, then Sam smiled broadly. He opened his arms and hurried toward her. "Glenda, congratulations, I'm so happy for you," he exclaimed as he hugged her.

"I'm sorry we left those pictures outside," Glenda said contritely. "That was mean."

"Don't you worry. I'm having my own private bonfire to get rid of them. I don't know whether you've heard . . ."

"I have," Glenda said.

"I'm so ashamed of myself. I let her nag me into not giving you bonuses. Come to my office, right now. I know you don't need it, but I wrote out the checks I should have given you last night. Glenda, you've been such a wonderful employee the last eighteen years. It's almost like you're my daughter." He hugged her again. "I won't be able to look myself in the mirror until those bonus checks are cashed."

"Mr. Conklin, that's very kind of you, but we can't take the time for that now." Glenda introduced Regan, then showed him Flower's picture. "Duncan's sure that she ran into trouble. You didn't see her in here today, did you?"

Sam studied the picture. "No, I didn't. Did you ask the others?" He nodded toward the front of the store.

"Yes, no one saw her, and no one remembers anyone asking for Duncan."

Quickly Sam showed the photo to everyone in the kitchen. The response was negative. "Do you have any idea what time she might have come in?" he asked as he handed Glenda back the picture.

"Our guess is some time after ten o'clock. That's the time her bus arrived at the station."

"The Skunk was still here then," Sam said. "I wonder if she saw her."

"The Skunk?" Glenda asked.

"Don't act dumb."

"Okay, I won't."

"I could call her if you want to see if she might have talked to Duncan's girlfriend. I'd only make a call to her for something like this."

"If you don't mind. This is important."

Not surprisingly, Rhoda didn't pick up the phone. "She's probably staring at my name on her cell phone right now cussing me out," Sam said. "Why don't you take her number and try her yourself? Maybe you'll have better luck."

But Rhoda Conklin didn't pick up when Regan tried her either. Regan left a message identifying herself and explaining the reason for her call. "Please get back to me as soon as possible."

Sam tapped his finger on the counter. "One of our new kids was working in produce this morning, and Rhoda tried to fire him. He's out loading the truck now." The back door opened. "Oh, here he comes. Hey, Zach," Sam called to the rosy-cheeked young man. "Come here for a minute, would you?"

"Sure, Mr. Conklin." Zach hurried over.

"No," he said, shaking his head when he looked at Flower's picture. "I haven't seen her. But I've got to tell you, she could have been standing in front of me, and I wouldn't have noticed with the way The Skunk kept yelling at me this morning. Mr. Conklin, I'm so glad you got rid of her," he said enthusiastically. "Give me a high five."

"Okay, Zach," Sam said, as he awkwardly raised his hand. "Keep loading the truck. The mayor's wife is getting nervous. We've got a town to feed."

"Yo." Zach picked up another completed tray and headed for the back door.

Glenda sighed. "Thanks, Mr. Conklin. We'd better get going. Duncan's pretty worried right now."

"Isn't it a shame that the day he learns his coworkers are handing him twelve million dollars, he ends up heartsick about his girlfriend? I hope it all works out. Duncan's a nice fellow."

"Maybe Flower's nearby and is going to surprise us all," Glenda suggested. "Hope to see you over the weekend, Mr. Conklin."

Out in the car, they had to tell an increasingly agitated Duncan that no one had seen Flower. "But it's been pretty busy in there today," Regan said, trying to sound positive. "Let's go to the bus depot."

"Everything's going wrong!" Duncan cried. "Alvirah just told me about the ring!" He looked out the window at the heavy clouds and the falling snow. "What if Flower suddenly had amnesia and is walking around in this weather?"

At the depot, Duncan insisted on coming inside. A cleaning woman was mopping the floor near the entrance. Regan showed her Flower's picture and explained why they were looking for her. The woman had only to glance at the picture before saying, "Yes, I saw her this morning. She was in the ladies' room gussying herself up when I went in there to empty the wastebaskets. A pretty little thing."

"You're sure it was her?" Duncan asked.

The woman frowned. "Either that or she was a dead ringer."

Poor choice of words, Regan thought. "Do you remember what she was wearing?"

"Nothing unusual. Blue jeans, I think. A ski jacket. Might have been gray. She had a red knapsack that had a slogan I hadn't seen in years. It said FLOWER POWER."

"That's definitely her," Duncan moaned.

"What time did you see her?" Regan asked the woman.

"I'd say it was around 10:30—right before my break."

The lone agent at the ticket counter had also noticed Flower. "I saw her get off the bus, and then I saw her leave the depot. She definitely hasn't been back," he informed them.

Duncan looked at Glenda and Regan. "She's got to be here somewhere. If I have to ring every doorbell in this town, I will." He turned, leaned on his crutches, and moving as quickly as the bulky cast would allow, made his way back to the car.

# 27

The one window in Jed's office, high on the wall at the back of the shed, had a shade that was pulled most of the way down. Looking up, Flower could tell the snow was falling rapidly. When they left her, Betty had turned out all the lights, and Jed had shut off his three computers. The room was cold even though they had left one space heater on. Otherwise I'd freeze to death, Flower thought, shivering.

In the semidarkness she had already familiarized herself with her surroundings. This place is unbelievable, she thought fearfully. No one would ever guess it existed. And no one would guess, looking at folksy Jed, that he had an operation like this going on either. Keys were hanging over the workbench. A row of files was padlocked. From where she was sitting, Flower could see a screen that showed the activity recorded by eight different security cameras around the bed and breakfast.

They said they had no TV, radio, or internet access, Flower remembered bitterly as she tried to pick at the knots that bound her wrists together behind her back. But she couldn't reach the knots with her fingers. And this gag is choking me, she thought. She tried to move her jaw, but that only made it harder to breathe. Calm down, she warned herself. But how can I? Even if Duncan gives them the ticket, they'll never let me go. I can identify all of them. My only chance is that if they get the ticket and are able to cash it and escape the country, they just might leave word where I could be found. That's never going to happen.

All of this is my fault, she thought. When I didn't hear from Duncan, I didn't worry for one single minute that something might have happened to him. Is he feeling that way about me right now? Probably not, Flower decided, as tears stung her eyes. He's so good. Even if I do get out of here, I wouldn't blame him if he never wanted to see me again.

On the screen she saw a car pull into the driveway to the left of the Inn and take the first parking space. Three women got out and scurried toward the front door. People will be coming for tea, Flower thought. Some of them may have to park back here near the shed. If I can move this lawn chair and start slamming it against the wall when a car pulls into one of the spots near the shed, I might attract someone's attention.

Slowly, tentatively, she began to lift herself and the chair upward from the floor, inching toward the wall. If this thing lands on its side, I'll never be able to get up, she told herself.

And they'll know I was trying to escape. So what? Heaving her body, she was able to move slowly, painfully across the cement floor. More cars were pulling into the driveway. She reached the wall just as a car pulled up outside the shed. It sounded so close. She heard the doors open and close.

"I tell you, Tishie," a woman said, her tone strident. "Sam Conklin misses me already. I knew he would. But I'm not picking up the phone for anyone. This is time for Rhoda."

"You're darn right," Tishie said.

Instinctively, Flower tried to scream but only a whimper-like sound came from her mouth. That must be Conklin's wife, she thought frantically. I'd recognize that voice anywhere. But maybe she can save me. With all her strength Flower hurled her body, tied to the lawn chair, against the wall.

"Rhoda, what was that noise?"

"I didn't hear anything. Come on, Tishie, I'm getting wet."

On the cement floor, Flower was struggling to right the chair and try again when she heard the door to Jed's office slide open.

# 28

These are the Festival of Joy oven mitts and potholders we'll be selling, starting this evening," Muffy explained to Nora, Luke, and Willy, as they walked through the heavily stocked sales area of the church basement. "Then we have water colors of Branscombe scenes, painted by our Red Barn artists. Red Barn is a haven for seniors who love to paint, and we have two professional artists who volunteer their time to teach a couple of times a week."

Nora examined the paintings carefully. "They're lovely," she said. "Several of them are really fine."

Luke, whose taste in art was more Georgia O'Keefe's style of painting, pretended to study the cozy scenes. Willy remembered that in the sixth grade, Sister Jane had labeled his "Keep Them Flying" poster of an airplane soaring past a flag as resembling "a flying fish wrapped in a rag." She was one tough old bird, he thought. She'd have found fault with the *Mona Lisa*. I'll buy the water color of the Branscombe Inn for Alvirah, he decided. She always likes a memento of places we've stayed.

Alvirah. Where the heck was she? And did she ever get any lunch? She'd been hungry enough on the plane to eat stale pretzels, then had dived into those chocolates he'd bought her at the convenience store. Last night, being hungry had landed her in the emergency room. Who knows what might happen if she got hungry today? He was tempted to call her cell phone, but he knew she'd get back to him when she was ready.

Luke had once suggested that Milton's line, "They also serve who only stand and wait," should be an inspiration to the two of them. Willy remembered he had asked, "Milton who?"

"Didn't the ladies do a beautiful job transforming the basement into a winter wonderland?" Muffy was asking.

"It is so pretty," Nora agreed. "I was raised in a small town in New Jersey, and it had the same feeling I'm experiencing here. Everyone enjoyed pitching in. In fact in our town, when a new parish was started, the men got together and renovated an old barn into a beautiful chapel."

"And a-one, and a-two, and a-three," a voice boomed from a side room.

Like a clap of thunder, a piano began to play, and a chorus of voices rang out, "Deck the halls with boughs of holly . . ."

"The choir's tuning up for this evening," Muffy explained. "Oh, here comes Steve."

They all turned to look as the Mayor of Branscombe

came down the stairs. Something's up, Luke thought as he observed the forced smile on Steve's face and his quick greetings to the Festival volunteers as he hurried across the room. "I just talked to Jack. Looks as if we have to get another search party organized," he said tersely. "Duncan Graham's girlfriend, Flower Bradley, came into town from California to surprise him this morning and is missing. We're having copies of her picture made to post around town. Then, besides searching the woods, we'll start ringing doorbells and making inquiries. She has to have been seen by *someone*."

Nora studied the expression of profound worry on Steve's face. "You haven't told us everything, Steve."

He looked around. There was no one standing within earshot. "Duncan phoned Flower's mother and found out something he never knew about her. When Flower turns twenty-five—which is next month—she comes into a trust fund that's worth a fortune. Her great-grandfather was the founder of Corn Bitsy Cereals. Now her mother is afraid that someone may have followed Flower here and may be holding her for ransom, but she doesn't want that to get out if at all possible."

"How much is the trust fund worth?" Luke asked.

"One hundred million plus."

"Jingle Bells, Jingle Bells," the choir was singing. "Jingle all the way."

# 29

Glenda's ex-husband, Harvey, met up with a reporter and a camera crew from BUZ outside the house he had shared with Glenda for twelve years. He had more than willingly agreed to a reenactment of his clothes being left on the driveway in trash bags and then run over by a delivery truck. Glenda had not been invited to participate.

With the promise of a full and better-quality replacement of his clothes by the network, Harvey brought along the new wardrobe that he had acquired after a judge ruled that Glenda's action had been malicious. As instructed, Harvey had stuffed the garments into two garbage bags.

"You think this weather is bad?" he asked as he got out of his van, dragging the bags. "This snow can't compare with the way it rained that day. It was terrible. Strong gusty winds. Glenda claimed it wasn't raining when she put the bags on the driveway, but give me a break. It didn't take a rocket scientist to realize the heavens were about to open up."

What a dope, Ben Moscarello, the reporter from BUZ

was thinking as he shook Harvey's hand. "Hello, Harvey. That must have been quite a day. Why don't you leave the bags here on the driveway? We'll get a shot of them with your clothes sticking out."

"It was very insulting. Glenda had no right to treat my stuff that way," Harvey said as he set the bags down, untwisted the ties, and started rummaging through the contents. With great care, he draped the sleeves of some of his favorite sweatshirts over the sides.

"That's the idea, Harvey," Ben said approvingly.

"I gave Glenda a suitcase for her birthday about four years ago. It wouldn't have killed her to pack my clothes nice and neat in it. I would have returned it."

Of *course* you would have, Ben thought sarcastically. "Now Harvey we want you to stand on the front porch and talk about the horror and embarrassment of driving down the block and suddenly seeing the wardrobe you took such pride in blown all over the road, wet, dirty, then covered with tire tracks."

"I'll never forget it as long as I live!" Harvey said. "*Never!* It still gives me nightmares."

"Save that for when the camera's running," Ben told him as they walked up the path to the house. "Harvey, we don't want to mention that you were late to pick up your gear. That wouldn't be sympathetic."

"I was only five minutes late!" Harvey protested as he positioned himself on the top step of the porch.

"I know, but don't mention it. None of this was your fault. The point is, the viewing public likes victims. They not only like them, they root for them. And there aren't too many victims the public will feel sorrier for than someone whose former spouse hits it big in the lottery."

Harvey's face fell. "I'll never get over it."

"Let's roll the camera," Ben said quickly. "Harvey, you say you're never going to get over this?"

"Never!"

"Would you say the humiliation of seeing your clothes strewn on the street made you depressed?"

"I was furious and depressed, and too broke to replace anything. Thank God the judge made Glenda pay up. I hadn't had gainful employment for about a year before we split. I'd been looking for work, then one day I went into a Go Go Bar and met Penelope and . . ."

"Harvey!" Ben interrupted. "We don't want to know that you didn't find a job because you were too busy with a girl-friend. That isn't sympathetic either."

"You want to know the worst part?" Harvey asked. "Right after the divorce went through, Penelope dumped me."

The cameraman tapped Ben on the shoulder. "We've got to get this scene moving. Right now we're supposed to be taking background shots of the church bazaar, then get over in time to catch Santa climbing into his sleigh."

"Okay," Ben said impatiently, then turned back to Harvey. "Let's pick up with your telling us that after twelve beautiful years you and Glenda split, and how shocked you were when she showed a side of her personality that was mean and vindictive."

"Vindictive?"

"She wasn't nice to you."

Harvey cleared his throat. "Glenda and I got married when she was twenty and I was twenty-four," he began. "She was no Marilyn Monroe, but I thought she was a very nice person. I was wrong."

"Cut!" an exasperated Ben moaned. "Harvey, get this straight. You start knocking your ex-wife's looks and every woman who watches the show will hate you. Stick to how much you loved her."

"I loved my wife," Harvey began dutifully. "I still love her. Glenda is A–number one in my book."

Keep going, Ben prayed.

"I begged her to work things out with me," Harvey continued, warming to his narrative. "But she coldly refused, and we were divorced. Glenda got the house, which I thought was very unfair, but since we had remortgaged it, there wasn't much equity, if you get my drift."

"Harvey," Ben interrupted. "Tell us about the clothes as you walk toward the driveway."

Harvey nodded. Dramatically he pointed at the front door of the house. "It was very unfriendly of Glenda to change the locks on the doors so fast. I hadn't had the chance to get all my stuff out. We agreed she'd leave my clothes out on the driveway." He walked over and pointed at the bags. "They couldn't have been here for two minutes when the storm blew in," he said, blinking as snow pelted his face.

"Good, Harvey," Ben said. "We're going to spread the clothes around the street now and have our truck run over them."

Five minutes later Harvey was standing on the road, looking down, tears in his eyes. "I couldn't believe that the woman I had shared twelve years of my life with could do this to me," he said, pointing at his soggy shirts and pants and sweaters and socks and underwear. "I was so crushed when I came upon this devastating scene. I was crushed worse than my clothes."

Ben made a signal with his arm. A truck came rumbling down the road and ran over Harvey's new wardrobe.

"Cut!" Ben called. "That's a wrap!"

Another segment of the Festival of Joy special was in the can.

# 30

Before Duncan called Flower's mother, they canvassed the stores along Main Street, just in case Flower had stopped in one of them. They even went to the movie theater in the hopes that she had gone there to kill time before surprising Duncan.

No one had seen her.

Then they called the Branscombe Inn and the two bed-and-breakfasts in town, the Hideaway and the Knolls. She hadn't registered at any of them. That was when Duncan reluctantly phoned Flower's parents. Her mother, Margo Bradley, whom he had never met, was surprised to hear from him.

"Duncan, hello. I tried to call Flower, but her phone is turned off and her mailbox is full. Is anything wrong?" Margo asked quickly.

With a heavy heart, Duncan told her what had happened.

"I was always afraid of this!" Margo cried.

"Why?"

"Flower is an heiress of the Corn Bitsy Cereal Company. Her great-great grandfather founded it. I've had a fear of her being kidnapped ever since she was born."

"An *heiress?*" Duncan had said in disbelief. "I'd never have guessed that in a million years."

"That's the way she wanted it," Margo explained anxiously. "She wanted to meet someone who would love her for herself."

"I do," Duncan said vigorously. "I'm just surprised because when she talked about her life growing up, it seemed just like mine."

"We didn't have a wealthy lifestyle," Margo explained. "Her father and I were never interested in money. I was allowed access to my trust fund at eighteen, and in the following five years ended up giving most of the money away to causes we supported and anyone who asked to borrow. That's why Flower isn't allowed near her trust until she's twenty-five. Our family has shunned publicity, but people know there's money. I'm so afraid, with her trust coming due, that someone might have targeted her."

"Mrs. Bradley, it might have nothing to do with her family money. I won twelve million dollars in the lottery last night, and there's been a lot of publicity about it. If she was targeted, it could have been because of *me*," he admitted.

"Duncan," Margo said impatiently, "Flower's trust is worth over 100 million dollars. I knew she shouldn't go flying across the country to spend time with a man she knows nothing about."

"I *love* Flower," Duncan protested. "And I won't let anything happen to her. I promise you. I will find her."

"Don't talk about her trust fund publicly. If Flower is okay and out there somewhere, let's not give some crazy the idea to try and find her on his own."

When Duncan hung up, he was distraught. Stumbling over his words, he told them what Flower's mother had just revealed.

"Duncan," Jack said. "We'll let Steve know Flower is missing and that it's urgent the police be on the lookout for her. We'll have to tell him why we suspect a serious problem. Otherwise he'll wonder why they're supposed to look for a twenty-four-year-old woman who has only been out of touch for a few hours."

As Jack called Steve, Alvirah thought about the time Willy was kidnapped and held for ransom. She had managed to get a job as a maid in a sleazy hotel where she believed he was being kept. The criminals who took him had planned to kill him once the ransom money was paid, she remembered. Thank God I was able to save him. Where could Flower be? The engagement ring intended for her was in Alvirah's purse. Alvirah realized she was getting one of her funny feelings. Could this ring lead them to Flower?

I've got to talk to the man who found the ring and brought it to the jewelry shop, she decided.

# 31

In the basement of The Hideaway, Woodrow and Edmund were sitting on a lumpy, dusty old couch that smelled of mildew. A lone lightbulb dangled overhead. Betty had given them a couple of blankets to throw over their legs. Even so, they were both cold and increasingly fearful of Jed and Betty's plans to get rid of Flower.

Edmund's head was in his hands. "Woodrow, I'm scared!" he said.

"Take it easy, Edmund, I'm nervous enough already. My stomach's a little off. I shouldn't have eaten all that candy."

"Woodrow, I don't care about your bellyache. We *can't* be involved in a murder. Did you see the look on that girl's face when we tied her up and left her back there? She's terrified, and she's just a kid."

"What are we going to do?" Woodrow asked angrily, spitting out the words. "Our only choice is to forget about the lottery ticket and drive out of town just the way we planned to do after our last class next week. We won't get the money, but we won't get arrested for murder either."

"We will be if we let Betty and Jed kill her, and we don't try to stop them. With or without us, they're not going to let that girl live." Edmund swallowed hard and ran his fingers through his thinning hair. "If only we had inherited a little money. We were never greedy with our scams. I really don't think we ever took money from that many people who couldn't afford to lose a few bucks."

"Shut up, Edmund. How about Duncan? We cleaned *him* out."

Overhead they could hear the floorboards creaking as Betty hurried back and forth from the kitchen to the living room. Tea time was obviously busy. "Jed," they heard her snap. "You forgot to put preserves on table four."

"She's *mean*," Edmund said, his voice shaking. "Woodrow, what are we going to do? We can't let that girl die. We're pretty bad, but we're not killers. Those two," he pointed toward the ceiling, "seem to have no problem with it. In prison the talk always was that Jed got away with a lot of really bad stuff. He was just stupid and got caught robbing a bank. With a loaded gun."

"What do you suggest?" Woodrow asked sarcastically.

"We get the girl out of here, then contact Duncan. She'll

be our witness that we saved her life. If he won't give us the ticket, we'll just head for the hills."

Woodrow was silent for a moment. "Edmund, how stupid are you? Betty and Jed will never let us get out of here alive with that girl. They probably have guns hidden away in Betty's baking pans. If they think their whole way of life is threatened, they won't be afraid to use them."

"Well then let's go for it while they're busy with their tea party."

"You think the girl's going to come willingly? No way."

"Believe me, Woodrow, she'll trust us more than Betty. If I had a choice of going with us, or staying here with Betty and Jed, I'd go with us."

"And if we save her life, the least Duncan can do is give us back our ticket," Woodrow agreed. "One good turn deserves another, as Aunt Millie aways told us."

Edmund snapped his fingers. "I know! Let's get Aunt Millie involved."

"How?"

"Have her get the ticket back from Duncan. She'll be outraged if she thinks we missed out on 180 million dollars. We'll explain to her we made a little mistake with the oil well, but that we plan to pay everyone back. She doesn't have to know anything about Flower. We'll just tell her to call Duncan and say that if he doesn't give her the lottery ticket she bought at the convenience store when she was visiting us, she'll be very hurt. And her nephews don't want to see her or anyone else hurt. Duncan would have to be an idiot if he doesn't get the message."

"He *is* an idiot."

"So what? I think it could work. We want Aunt Millie to stay completely innocent about Flower. We'll get away from here with Flower, in Jed's van, and head to Canada. I saw Jed's keys on a hook in the shed. No one will be on the look-out for his van—he wouldn't dare report it missing. We'll tell Millie to hire a limo and head to Branscombe. She could be in town by ten o'clock. As soon as we get word she has the ticket in her hot little hands, we'll release Flower."

"And I guess if we get caught, we can comfort ourselves with the thought that there will be some family money when we finally get out of prison," Woodrow said glumly.

"If she doesn't spend it all first."

Woodrow shrugged, as if defeated. "At least we'll know we did the right thing, saving Flower's life."

"Let's call Aunt Millie real fast," Edmund said. "I want to get that girl out of here."

Aunt Millie was on Woodrow's speed dial. Not surprisingly, she answered on the first ring.

"Woodrow, to what do I owe this honor?" she asked crisply. "It's always good to hear from you, but it usually means something's up."

"Edmund and I wanted to see how you were," Woodrow said innocently.

"Bored to tears. I can't go back to the casino until I get

my social security check. Life is a drag when you don't have money. So what do you want?"

"Actually, we have sad news and glad news."

"Fire away."

"We bought a lottery ticket and won 180 million dollars."

"What! I don't believe it! What could possibly be the sad news?"

"We were in the middle of running a scam and . . ."

"You two never learn do you?"

"Listen, we were smart enough to win the lottery."

"That's true."

"But someone stole the ticket from our freezer, and we want you to get it back. We're sure we know who it is. His name is Duncan Graham and wouldn't you know, we sold him stock in a phony oil well."

"You make my head spin. Why on earth would he give it back to me?"

Woodrow hesitated. "He's already in on the other winning ticket that was sold in this lottery so he's getting twelve million dollars anyway. But he stole our ticket and he knows it. We just want to convince him the ticket is yours. And we want him to be afraid that if he doesn't give it to you, the rightful owner, who bought the ticket when you visited your two loving nephews the other day, he'll be sorry. Got it?"

"Oh, what a good idea! Trust me, I know what to do. I get a third, right?"

Woodrow gulped. "Of course, Aunt Millie. We'll even pay for your limo up to Branscombe."

"Give me Duncan's number . . ."

When Woodrow snapped his cell phone closed, he looked at his cousin. "We're lucky to have her," he said to Edmund. "Even if she is a little greedy and wants a third."

"Two-thirds of a loaf is better than none," Edmund replied. "Let's get out of here."

# 32

"What do you think you're doing?" Betty asked harshly as she pulled Flower's chair upright. "Trying to get help? That's not a good idea. You might be interested to know I got a call to see if you registered here. Maybe your boyfriend didn't intend to dump you after all."

Betty yanked open the drawer of the computer desk and pulled out a thick roll of black duct tape. She dragged the chair to the desk and with quick strokes bound the chair and desk together. Looking down into Flower's terrified eyes, she said, "If you know what's good for you, you won't try anything like that again." She then took a dish towel out of the deep pocket of her apron and blindfolded Flower. "See no evil," she muttered irritably. "I've got to get back to the tea."

She's going to kill me, Flower thought, as the door slid closed. This is the end. Desperately she strained to free herself.

A few minutes later the door slid open again. Oh my God, Flower thought. She's going to kill me now.

Then one of the financial advisers who had helped tie her up said quietly, "Don't be scared, Flower. We're getting you out of here. All we want is our lottery ticket back from your boyfriend. Those two intend to kill you, and we're not going to let it happen."

"Oh, you're not, are you?" Betty cried.

"Huh?" the man said in a panic.

A few seconds later Flower heard his body land with a thud on the cement floor.

# 33

Steve wants us to bring Flower's picture over to the church bazaar," Jack said. "We can make copies of it there. He says there are a lot of people around. We can show the photo to all of them. It's a good place to start."

These roads are getting slippery, Duncan worried, and with each passing minute it's getting darker. How can this have happened? he asked himself. How? If only I had just stayed home last night.

It's the calm before the storm with the way some of the streets are deserted, Alvirah thought. Everyone's probably getting ready for the candlelight ceremony and Santa's ride through the snow. But then she saw that the church parking lot was almost full. Jack stopped at the front door. Glenda and Regan jumped out to assist Duncan, who was unsteady on his crutches.

"Jack, I'll keep you company while you park," Alvirah offered.

"Alvirah, that's crazy."

"Please, just park the car. I've got to make a phone call."

When Regan closed the door, Alvirah said, "Jack, I didn't want to say this in front of Duncan. I want to follow up on that man who found the flower ring. It's possible that companion who very likely killed Mrs. O'Keefe's friend Kitty is around here somewhere. And there's always the wild chance that somehow Flower met up with her. If that companion is here, I'm sure she's following the lottery story."

"It's certainly worth checking out," Jack agreed. "That ring didn't walk to Branscombe."

But there was still no answer at Rufus Blackstone's home. "Why doesn't he have an answering machine?" Alvirah grumbled. "In this day and age . . . Let me try Mrs. O'Keefe. I just want to see what she remembers about the companion. She's probably mad at me because I haven't talked to her in so long."

"No one could stay mad at you, Alvirah," Jack said amiably as he pulled into a parking space.

Alvirah began to dial. "I never forget a phone number," she bragged. "Particularly Bridget O'Keefe's. She was always calling me and leaving messages asking if I had seen her glasses or her keys or her address book. . . . Hello, Bridget? This is Alvirah Meehan . . ." She laughed. "No, I'm not too big for my britches. I *do* want to see you for lunch one of these days . . . But the strangest thing happened today. I'm in a little town in New Hampshire, and I spotted Kitty's flower ring in a jewelry shop window. I'm absolutely *sure* it was hers."

On the other end of the phone, Alvirah's former employer, who had been watching her afternoon soap operas, gasped. "That ring has been on my mind lately. How did the jeweler get it?"

"A local man found it. I'm trying to get in touch with him. I wanted to see what you remembered about Kitty's companion. I only saw her once from a distance."

Mrs. O'Keefe lowered the volume on the television. "I still feel so terrible about Kitty. That companion, who we later found out used a fake name, was syrupy sweet in the beginning, then she started to boss Kitty around."

"I remember you were worried about that. But what did she *look* like?"

"She had one of those round faces that always had a phony smile plastered on it. Brown hair. Medium sized, but kind of a big frame. She pretended to act concerned about Kitty and was always saying she wanted to fatten Kitty up. It bugged Kitty, who said the companion's head was always in and out of the oven, baking cakes and cookies, most of which she ate herself. To think she got away with robbing poor Kitty blind, then pushing her down the stairs. We both know she did that. Alvirah, if you find her, I'd love to get the chance to spit in her face."

"Bridget, I would love to find her. Kitty was such a sweet

lady. I'll call you when I get back to New York. I have the ring. As long as Kitty's nephew says it's okay, it's yours. I heard Kitty say so many times that she wanted you to have it."

"Oh, Alvirah, I can't believe how good you are. The ring won't bring Kitty back, but it will make me feel close to her again."

Alvirah said her good-byes and closed her cell phone. "That wasn't much help," she admitted. "The murdering companion likes to bake. Which reminds me, I'm hungry." She reached in her purse for a chocolate caramel. "Jack would you like one?"

"Sure," he said. As he unwrapped the red and green foil he asked, "Alvirah, how's your head feeling?"

Alvirah opened the car door. "I'll think about it when we get Flower back."

Jack put his hand under her arm as they walked carefully through the parking lot. Inside the church, they went down the steps to the basement, which was cheerfully decorated and abuzz with smiling volunteers. They could hear the choir rehearsing nearby. "Nine ladies dancing, eight maids a-milking, seven swans a-swimming, six geese a-laying . . ."

Alvirah turned to Jack. "Five gooolden rings," she sang off-key.

"Jack!"

They both turned. Regan was hurrying toward them. "Duncan just got a phone call from the Winthrops' elderly aunt. They know Duncan has the lottery ticket. She said he'd better not cash it because it belongs to her, and she wants it back or she'll be very hurt."

"Hurt?" Jack repeated.

"That's what she said. Duncan is sure it's a threat and that those guys have Flower, but the aunt hung up before he could question her."

"How is he supposed to get the ticket to her?" Alvirah asked.

"She said she'd call back later. Duncan knows she didn't buy the ticket, but he doesn't care. He's going to give it to her anyway."

Alvirah's heart sank. She'd been hoping against hope that Flower had maybe gone skiing for the day and was going to surprise Duncan tonight. These kidnapping situations usually don't end well, she thought. There's always the fear the kidnappers will panic, and then . . .

She knew that Regan and Jack were thinking the same thing.

# 34

You two-timing jerk!" Betty cried as she stood over a stunned Edmund, whom she'd karate chopped in the back of the head. Dazed, he began to struggle clumsily to his feet.

"Don't bother," Jed said quietly from the doorway, pointing a pistol at Edmund. "Betty, let's get him tied up."

"What do you think I'm doing?" she asked impatiently, grabbing the duct tape. "I've got to get back inside. People are wolfing down my scones." With swift movements she secured Edmund's hands behind his back and twisted tape around his legs.

They heard the outer door of the shed open and close. "Here comes 911," Jed scoffed in a low voice.

As Betty was about to stuff Edmund's mouth, he cried out, "Woodrow, run!"

But it was too late.

A moment later Jed was escorting Woodrow back to his

office, his gun pointed at Woodrow's ear. "Betty, it looks like you're going to have to help me up at Devil's Pass. We now have three people going for a dip tonight."

"Jed, what are you talking about?" Woodrow asked, his voice trembling.

"Your cousin here said you wanted to let this little girl go. That wouldn't have been so good for me and Betty, now would it?"

"We weren't going to let her go."

"Then what were you planning to do?" Betty asked harshly as she pulled his arms behind him and started to bind them with the tape.

"Let's work this out," Woodrow pleaded. "When we cash in the lottery ticket, we'll only take ten percent. The rest is yours."

"Only if you throw in a couple oil wells," Betty snapped. "I'm tired of listening to your lies." She stuffed his mouth with a gag.

Within five minutes, their three captives securely bound and gagged, Betty was back in the parlor.

Rhoda Conklin and Tishie Thornton were talking animatedly to two women at a neighboring table.

"They actually put Duncan's girlfriend's ring on display at Pettie's jewelry store," Tishie was telling her enthralled listeners. "He was furious."

"Some girl came into the store looking for him this

morning," Rhoda said. "I don't see how that could be his girlfriend though. She seemed stunned when I told her he'd quit because he won the lottery."

One of the women waved her hand dismissively. "Maybe it was someone who did know he had won and was hoping to meet him."

"But who would go to work when they just came into twelve million dollars?" the other woman asked. She laughed. "Right, Rhoda?"

"It's not my problem anymore who does or doesn't come to work," Rhoda snarled. "Or who Duncan's girlfriend is."

They don't know she's missing yet, Betty thought gratefully as she started to clear a vacated table. We have to get Flower and the others out of here the minute it gets dark. Rhoda spotted her and beckoned. "Could we have our check now? I was wondering where you were. We would have liked another cup of tea, but it's too late now. I even went looking for you in the kitchen."

Did she look into the laundry room? Betty wondered uneasily. She had stuffed Flower's coat in the hamper and tossed her knapsack behind it. Could Rhoda have seen it? "Sorry," Betty said with a smile. "Things have been so busy with the Festival. I've had my hands full."

"We don't care about the Festival," Tishie said. "Bah, humbug."

"Bah, humbug is right," Rhoda agreed as she reached for her purse. "This is my treat, Tishie. Thanks for picking me up. I knew I couldn't drive in this mess. Thank God I'm moving back to Boston tomorrow."

Thank God is right, Betty thought.

# 35

After the lottery ticket was securely locked away in the vault of Branscombe's only bank, Ralph, Tommy, and Marion agreed to meet at the start of the candlelight ceremony. Ralph and Judy, hand in hand, had headed toward their car; Tommy, closely guarded by his parents, had gotten behind the wheel of their ten-year-old sedan; Marion had driven home through the snow by herself.

Inside her house, Marion put the keys on the kitchen counter and went into her bedroom. I'll get out of my dress-up clothes and put a robe on, she thought. I'll make myself a cup of tea and relax for a few hours. I hardly closed an eye last night, but I know I'll never sleep now.

Out of the blue, she burst into tears. Grabbing a hanky from her drawer, she dabbed her eyes. I feel so alone, she thought. This money is wonderful, but I'm going to miss seeing my friends every day—the people I worked with, excluding The Skunk, and our regular customers. What am I going to *do* with myself when I wake up in the morning?

She put on her robe, tied the sash, and told herself how silly she was being. So many people would give their eyeteeth to be in my shoes right now, she thought. But if only Gus were still alive. We'd have so much fun planning trips. She remembered the dozens of pictures of penguins a Conklin's customer had shown her, taken on a cruise to Antarctica. I think Gus and I would have skipped the penguins and gone to someplace warm, Marion decided wistfully.

In the kitchen, she turned on the kettle, opened the cabinet, got out a cup and a tea bag. I should call Glenda. Reaching for the phone, she looked at the list of numbers taped to the side of the refrigerator and dialed. When Glenda answered, Marion could hear the buzz of activity in the background. "Glenda, the ticket is locked up," she began brightly. "How's Duncan?"

"Not good," Glenda said quickly. "His girlfriend is missing."

"What?"

Glenda filled her in. "I'm at the church bazaar. We're showing her picture to everyone. On top of that, we picked up the flower ring from the jewelry store, and it turns out it was stolen eight years ago."

"Flower's ring was stolen?"

"Actually, what I mean is that the ring Duncan bought for her is in the shape of a flower, and . . . I'm sorry, Marion, I can't talk now."

"I want to help!" Marion cried.

"We can't have you walking around in the snow ringing doorbells."

"Glenda, don't put me out to pasture! Don't forget, until this morning I stood on my feet all day at the bakery."

"I know what you can do. I'll have someone here e-mail you Flower's picture. Go down to Conklin's, stand inside the entrance, and show it to everyone who comes in. Maybe someone saw her."

"Conklin's?" Marion asked tentatively.

"Oh, I didn't tell you. The Skunk is gone for good. She and Sam broke up this morning. He's thrilled."

"Send me that e-mail ASAP. I'm on my way!" Marion hung up. A flower-shaped ring, she thought as she rushed back into the bedroom. I know I've seen somebody wearing one.

But who?

And where?

# 36

Betty carried the last tray of tea cups and dessert plates into the kitchen. She dropped the tray next to the sink and with heavy steps strode to the door of the laundry room.

"What are you doing?" Jed asked.

"Checking to see if that knapsack is visible. Rhoda Conklin was in the kitchen when we were in the shed. She saw Flower this morning at the market, and she may have noticed she was carrying a red knapsack." Betty stared at the red fabric sticking up from behind the hamper. "You can see a little bit of it, but not so much that you'd pay attention. If that 'Flower Power' logo had been visible, we could have been sunk." She grabbed the knapsack and Flower's coat and threw them at Jed. "Pull the van up next to the shed and hide these in it. We've got to move the three of them into the van and off this property fast."

"Betty, it's not dark yet."

"Jed, stop being so stupid. Rhoda Conklin, that gossip Tishie Thornton, and some other women were all talking about Flower. They don't know that she's missing yet, but I'm sure word has gotten out. Someone's already called here to see if she checked in. We can't take a chance that the police may stop by and start snooping around. They don't need a search warrant to walk around the back and see the Winthrops' car behind the shed. Let me remind you—they told us the cops were probably looking for them."

"Keep your voice down," Jed snapped. "Someone may be upstairs."

"No one is upstairs. Why would the television people be here when they have the Festival to cover?" she snapped back.

"Betty, we have to wait until it gets dark," he said firmly. "It'll only be another half hour."

"Then just pull the van around and stay with them in the shed until we leave. That girl is smart. She already figured out a way to attract attention. Someone could have heard her kicking the wall if I hadn't stopped her."

"So, you stopped her. But remember, this is *your* fault. You should have handled it better when the Winthrops showed up."

"And you should never have become friends with them in prison!" Nervously, Betty began to rinse the cups. "Jed, after we get rid of them we'd better think about moving on from here, and soon. There are going to be a lot of questions asked when Flower doesn't show up, never mind the other two. If anyone starts digging deep, it won't take them long to find out that the real Betty and Jed Elkins died when their touring bus crashed in Germany six years ago."

# 37

Duncan, if you perceive that woman's call as being a threat, then you might be right that those guys have Flower," Jack said bluntly.

"We'd better talk in the office," Steve suggested. "It's through that door in the corner."

Steve and Muffy, the Reillys, Alvirah and Willy, and Glenda and Duncan followed Steve into the office, and Jack closed the door behind them.

"They must have Flower," Duncan blurted. "That's why I'm going to give that ticket to their aunt. Why did she hang up? I didn't say I wouldn't give her the ticket."

"She's playing with you, Duncan," Regan said. "She knows exactly what she's doing."

Duncan pointed to the window. "It's going to be dark soon. I can't just sit around and wait for that woman to call back. We've got to look for Flower. It may sound stupid to you, but I feel as if she's pleading with me to find her before it's too late."

"We will, Duncan," Jack said quickly. "But we can't officially treat this as a kidnapping yet. You did take the ticket they bought, and they want it back. It could be just a coincidence that Flower is missing. And her disappearance could involve someone else, now that we know she's an heiress. The thing you have to take heart about is that she's an adult, and hasn't been out of touch for all that long. She tried to reach you a few times this morning. She could walk in the door of this bazaar any minute."

"That's not going to happen," Duncan said flatly. "I know she's out there, and I know she needs my help."

"Well then let's get started," Regan said briskly. "Steve, can we use one of these machines to duplicate Flower's picture?"

"Yes."

"This is where we've been doing the mailings for the Festival," Muffy informed them. "I'll scan the picture into the computer and print out copies. Then we can do an e-mail blast. We must have the e-mail address of almost everyone in town. I'll send out an emergency alert, with Flower's picture and description."

"That'd be great," Regan said.

"I promised Marion I'd send her Flower's picture," Glenda said. "She's going to go over to Conklin's and show it to everyone who comes through the door."

"I'll call our chief of police," Steve said. "We reserve a few numbers that we use for emergencies. He'll give me one of them to put on the e-mail, so people can call in if they've seen her."

Duncan hadn't let go of Flower's picture since Glenda gave it back to him after they had canvassed Main Street. Now he carefully took the picture out of the frame and handed it to Muffy. She sat down at the computer and got to work.

The activity obviously sparked a flicker of hope in Duncan.

"Duncan, we'll show her picture to all the volunteers here now," Alvirah said comfortingly. "Then we'll take to the streets. There's no reason we can't reach everyone in Branscombe in the next hour."

"Steve and I are heading over to the park in a few minutes," Muffy said as the printer was spitting out copies of Flower's picture. "We're supposed to be at the reviewing stand when Santa arrives. We'll get some of the Festival workers over there to distribute Flower's picture."

"Aren't there going to be people lining Santa's route?" Nora asked.

"Yes," Steve answered. "They're gathering already. Some people don't mind waiting in the cold and snow to get a good view."

"Luke and I would be happy to go out along the route with Flower's picture and show it to the people who are already out there."

"Absolutely," Luke confirmed. He put his hand on

Duncan's shoulder but didn't know what to say. He remembered how terrified he had been when he and his driver were kidnapped and left to die in a leaky boat. "Let's move fast, everyone," he urged.

"I'll go with you and Nora," Willy offered. "I might not look it, but I'm quick on my feet. I know Alvirah will want to stay close to Regan and Jack and Duncan. It's best if we fan out and cover as much ground as possible."

"Muffy, before we all split up," Alvirah said, "do you know Rufus Blackstone?"

"Rufus Blackstone? Of course I do. He's playing Scrooge in 'A Christmas Carol.' They were rehearsing across the street at town hall, but they should be about wrapped up by now. Why?"

"I've been trying to reach him for the last couple of hours. He found the ring that Duncan bought for Flower. I wanted to ask him about it. It turns out it was stolen years ago. Leave no stone unturned," she said.

Regan looked at Alvirah. "I'll go over there with you right now," she said. She turned to Jack. "We'll be back in a few minutes. Why don't you and Glenda and Duncan show the pictures to the volunteers here?"

"Good idea."

They all left the office together, armed with stacks of Flower's picture. Steve beckoned to a male volunteer. "I need you to drop these people," he pointed to Luke and Nora, "along Santa's route."

"Sure, Mr. Mayor."

"And if you could drop this other gentleman at the halfway point to the park."

Regan and Alvirah hurried out of the church and across the street. The rehearsal had ended. Quickly they showed Flower's picture to the last actors who were on their way out the door.

"Sorry," they all said.

"I'd like to talk to Rufus Blackstone," Alvirah told them. "Is he still here?"

"He's the tall guy with the white hair and beard helping his wife on with her coat over there. They're talking to the director. Rufus always has a few suggestions at the end of every rehearsal."

"Mr. Blackstone!" Alvirah bellowed. "I need to speak to you."

Seeing the displeased look on his face, Alvirah and Regan hurried over to him and introduced themselves. "We're friends of the young man who bought the flower ring you found."

"You mean Duncan? Everyone's talking about him. He was missing all night and then won the lottery, right?"

"Yes, he did," Alvirah said quickly. "Mr. Pettie said you found the ring on the street."

"That's right."

"Where did you find it?"

He squinted. "Why do you want to know that?"

"Because it may have been dropped by the person who stole it eight years ago."

"My word!" Rufus's wife, Agatha, said. "It was stolen?"

"Yes," Alvirah answered. "And by someone who may be responsible for the death of the woman who owned it."

"Well, no wonder no one answered my lost-and-found ad in the paper," Rufus said. "I had it in there for weeks. I figured some tourist must have lost it."

"Lost it where?" Regan asked.

"In front of Conklin's market."

"Conklin's Market?" Alvirah repeated. "That place has seen a lot of action lately."

"The band on the ring was old and had broken. It may have split and fallen off someone's finger."

"Someone who shouldn't have been wearing it," Alvirah said, thinking of Kitty's companion.

Agatha's mouth was now agape. "I had joked with Rufus that Scrooge was a perfect role for him. He didn't want to let me have the ring. He wanted to sell it for whatever he could get. I'm kinda glad now, huh? Who wants to wear a ring that was on the finger of a murderer? Not me. Right, Rufus?"

"I suppose. Let's get going. We want to make the opening ceremony. Although what we should be doing is having another rehearsal. This play isn't ready for public viewing."

"I know you want to get going," Regan said quickly. "But if you could just take a look at this picture for a minute. It's

Duncan's girlfriend. She's been missing since this morning. You didn't happen to see her anywhere today, did you?"

"Nope," Rufus said brusquely after glancing at the photo.

Agatha scrunched up her eyes and studied the picture. Her jaw dropped even further. "Ohhh. Ohhhh. Wait just a minute. Ohhh. Yes, I did see her."

"Where?" Regan and Alvirah cried together.

"The poor little thing was crying. I passed her on Main Street. She was going one way, and I was going the other. I'd just come out of the beauty parlor."

"Did you see where she went?" Alvirah asked.

"I turned around because I wanted to see if I could help her. She seemed so upset. But she ducked down the alley. I couldn't have kept up with her if I tried. Besides, Rufus is always telling me to mind my own business!"

"Where exactly is the alley?" Regan asked.

"It's between Conklin's and the beauty parlor. You can't miss it. It's the only one there."

"We can't thank you enough," Regan said.

Alvirah was already racing out the door.

# 38

Warmly dressed in a sweater, slacks, snow boots, and a parka, Marion opened the door of Conklin's and looked around to see if she could spot Sam. The market was crowded with last minute shoppers. She was greeted with smiles and congratulations from all sides.

"If you're looking for Mr. Conklin, he's in the kitchen," Paige the cashier called to her. "Glenda stopped in before. Did you hear about Duncan's girlfriend?"

"That's why I'm here. I want to show her picture to the customers as they come in, but first I have to let Mr. Conklin know what I'm doing."

Marion walked back past the bakery and was startled to see that the shelves in the glass case were nearly empty. Lisa, the kid who assisted her at the counter, looked exhausted. She was ringing up a sale of the last two corn muffins and an apple tart.

The customer who reached out to take the package, a young woman in her twenties, was wearing a wide gold wedding ring. Marion stared at it. This is where I noticed the flower ring, she remembered excitedly. It was when I was handing someone her purchase. But who was it? Maybe it will come back to me.

In the kitchen, Marion was surprised to see Sam's son, Richard, slicing a ham. She'd known him since he was a little boy. "Marion," he said happily. "You spent all your money already?" He hurried over.

"Richard," she said, hugging him. "You look wonderful. I really meant to come see you in your play."

"That's okay. You can come to see the next one with Dad. I guess you heard he's flying solo."

"Yes," Marion said, blushing as Sam turned and spotted them. He looked tired but happy as he took her hands in his. "Marion this place isn't the same without you," he said heartily. "I told Glenda I have your bonus checks."

"Sam, please don't worry about that now," Marion said. "I was wondering if you'd mind if I stand at the front door and hand out Duncan's girlfriend's picture. She hasn't shown up yet, and he's terribly upset."

"Please," Sam said, still holding her hands in his. "Stay as long as you want."

Marion quickly posted herself just inside the entrance of the store. As she handed out Flower's picture, she kept thinking about the flower ring and how she had seen it on a customer's hand at her bakery counter. Think, Marion, she urged herself. It could be very important. She remembered how shy she was when she was a young girl. In the seventh grade when she was called on, she'd get flustered and everything would go out of her mind. Mrs. Griner, her English teacher, had been so understanding. She'd say, "Marion, you know the answer. Give yourself a minute to think. It will come to you."

It always did. But it's not coming to me now. I guess it's my age. I've done so many crossword puzzles to keep my brain sharp, she thought with frustration.

I've *got* to remember who was wearing that ring!

# 39

We'll retrace her steps," Jack said quickly. "I'll pull the car around."

"Flower was crying. Oh God!" Duncan moaned as he labored, on crutches, up the steps from the church basement to the outside.

"Main Street will be closed off by now," Glenda said when they got in the car. "That alley leads out to a tiny little street. That bed and breakfast I phoned, The Hideaway, is there. But the woman who owns it said Flower wasn't registered."

Regan and Alvirah looked at each other. "Let's go directly there," Regan said. "Maybe she registered under a different name."

"You think that's a possibility?" Duncan asked hopefully. "The owners of that place, Betty and Jed Elkins, are regular customers of Conklin's."

"It's worth a try," Regan said. "We'll start there."

Jack drove carefully through the snowy streets as Glenda directed him.

"People like to go to The Hideaway for tea," she said. "We're almost there. Take the next right."

They turned down a narrow road. On the left was a row of high hedges. "Those hedges hide the parking lot behind the stores. Up here to the left is the alley," Glenda explained. "It's almost directly opposite The Hideaway."

Jack parked the car in front of the Inn. "Glenda, this is your territory. Why don't you and I check the alley?"

"Alvirah and I will run inside and see what we can find out," Regan said.

"I'm coming with you," Duncan insisted.

"Duncan, we'll move faster if you wait here. Look at all those steps to the porch. Sit in the car with your cell phone on, and see if the Winthrops' aunt calls back," Regan suggested.

"All right, Regan," Duncan agreed, as he leaned back wearily against the seat.

# 40

Flower was wedged between Edmund and Woodrow in the back of Jed's van. Together Jed and Betty had carried each of them out of the shed and covered them with blankets. Flower's gag was so tight that she couldn't utter a sound, but both men were trying desperately to call for help through their taped mouths. The only sounds they managed to make were muted whimpers that no one outside the van could possibly hear.

I'm never going to see Duncan again, Flower thought.

"Come on, Betty," Jed said impatiently.

"I have to put a sign at the front desk that we're out at the candlelight ceremony and will be back later."

"You didn't do that yet?"

"No, Jed, I was too busy having my nails done," Betty retorted. "Get in the car. I'll be right back." She went in the kitchen door in time to hear the bell ring and the sound of the front door opening.

Oh no, she thought. But at least I didn't put the note out yet. I don't want anyone to see us driving away.

"This place feels deserted," Regan said as they waited at the registration desk. Then they heard heavy footsteps coming down the hall. A large woman was coming toward them with a welcoming smile.

"Hello, there. What I can I do for you nice ladies?"

"Are you Betty Elkins?" Regan asked.

"Yes, I am."

Regan handed her the flyer with Flower's picture. "We called before," she said. "This young woman, Flower Bradley, is still missing. We wondered if by any chance she registered here under a different name."

Betty pretended to study Flower's picture. "I'm so terribly sorry I can't help you, but I haven't seen her at all. And as I explained to Glenda, when she called before, we've been fully booked for weeks. No one could have walked in this morning and booked a room." With a sympathetic smile, she handed the flyer back to Regan. "What a shame. She looks like a lovely girl. I hope everything turns out all right."

Regan noticed that Betty Elkins was perspiring and seemed out of breath. "Would you mind keeping the picture and showing it to your other guests?"

"I wouldn't mind at all."

Neither Regan or Alvirah wanted to leave. They both

sensed the acute anxiety that Betty Elkins was trying to hide. I've never seen a phonier smile in my life, Alvirah thought.

"I hear that you serve wonderful teas every day," Regan said, stalling for time.

"You must come to one. I'm proud to say my scones are delicious, and I'm told I make a mean chocolate cake. Now if you'll excuse me, I have something on the stove."

Alvirah could almost hear Bridget O'Keefe's voice. ". . . she had a round face with a phony smile plastered on it. Her head was always in and out of the oven, baking cookies and cakes. . . . She ate most of them herself . . ." Alvirah looked from Betty's round face to the mechanical Santa on the reception desk, waving and bowing. Bridget O'Keefe was always telling me I must have thrown out her mechanical Santa by mistake. I always told her she'd open a drawer some day and find it. "This Santa is so cute," Alvirah began. "I had a friend, Kitty Whalen, who came to visit the woman I worked for . . ."

Alvirah noticed the twitch in Betty's cheek as Betty interrupted her. "I'm so sorry," Betty said, "but I do have to get back to the kitchen. And I'd like to be at the park when the candlelight ceremony begins."

"Thanks for your time," Regan said. As she and Alvirah reluctantly turned to go, the front door burst open, and Glenda rushed in, her eyes wide with excitement.

"Marion just called! Betty, maybe you can help us. Marion remembers seeing you wearing a flower ring. Of course you wouldn't have realized it was stolen. I mean, if it's the same one that Duncan bought . . ."

Alvirah's head swiveled around to Betty. Their eyes met. The smiling mask had been replaced by a look of malevolent fury. In one quick move, Betty overturned the desk and pushed it at them. As they jumped back, Betty ran down the hall with astonishing speed.

"You killed Kitty Whalen!" Alvirah shouted after her.

Regan climbed over the desk and ran down the hall, Alvirah a few steps behind her. When they reached the kitchen, it was empty, but the back door was open. They could hear the sound of a car tearing out of the driveway.

Alvirah's eyes caught sight of crumpled red and green foil candy wrappers on the counter. It was the same as the wrapper on the candy Willy had bought for her at the convenience store—the convenience store where the other lottery ticket had been bought by the financial crooks. The guy at the store had told her he had hardly sold any of them. "Regan!" she cried as she scooped up the scraps of foil. "Those financial advisers who we think have Flower might have been here. Maybe they're in cahoots with Betty!"

They raced back down the hall and out the front door. Glenda had run across the street to the alley to get Jack.

"In the car!" he shouted. "We can't lose them!"

# 41

"What happened, Betty?" Jed screamed as he floored the accelerator and raced out of the driveway past Jack's car. "While I was waiting for you I heard some guy yelling Flower's name."

"O'Keefe's cleaning lady recognized me."

"What?" Driving at a reckless speed, he turned left at the end of their block.

"Which way are we going?" Betty asked, her voice panicky as the wheels of the van began to slide. "They're following us."

"Be quiet! I found out which streets they're closing off and figured out the fastest way up to Devil's Pass."

Half choked under the stuffy blankets, Flower felt for the first time that there might be hope. She had heard Duncan calling her name. He had to be in the car that was following them. Keep up with us, she prayed.

Edmund wished he could comfort Flower. Who could believe this started with me and Woodrow winning the lottery? he asked himself.

Jed made a sharp left. The rear tires skidded, but he

managed to keep control. "We'll take this road straight out," he told Betty as he looked in the rear view mirror. "I think we lost them."

"Jed, be careful!" Betty screamed as the road curved to the right. Their headlights shone on an unexpected road block. Santas on horse-drawn sleighs could be seen everywhere. As a special surprise for the Festival of Joy, Santas from all over the state of New Hampshire had gathered in Branscombe and were now ready to participate in the opening ceremony.

Jed slammed on the brakes. The van spun around three times and slid to the side of the road. The troopers at the roadblock hurried over as the Reillys' car pulled up behind the Elkins's van.

"Careful, they may be armed," Jack shouted as he jumped out of the car.

Guns drawn, the troopers surrounded the van. The driver's door opened, and Jed, his hands up, stepped out onto the snowy road. At the same time, Betty opened the passenger door. "The gun is in the glove compartment, and there are folks in the back," she said bitterly.

Jack pulled open the back door of the van. He and Regan yanked away the blankets. Three people were struggling to free themselves. They had been blindfolded, gagged, and tied up.

"She's here, Duncan," Regan cried as she jumped in, pulled off Flower's blindfold, and untied her gag.

"Flower!" Duncan cried as he hobbled toward them.

Jack lifted Flower out and set her on her feet, holding her upright as a trooper cut the twine that bound her hands and feet.

"Oh, Duncan," Flower said weakly. "I wanted to surprise you."

"You sure did," Duncan cried. He dropped his crutches and threw his arms around her.

"I thought I'd never see you again," Flower whispered as he held her tight. Then she began to giggle as the troopers pulled the Winthrops out of the van. "Hey, Duncan, here are your financial advisers. Do you have any questions for them now that you finally won the lottery?"

Duncan laughed. "No! And I'm never going to reuse a plastic bag again." He brushed Flower's hair back from her forehead. "And I don't need any more of their advice to plan my life. The only thing I want to plan now is our wedding. Will you marry me, Flower?"

"As soon as possible."

Alvirah wiped a tear from her eye. "Isn't that beautiful?" she asked Regan and Glenda. "I hope they invite us to the wedding."

The roadblock was being pushed aside. "Time to get this show on the road," one of the cops called. As horses neighed and shook snow from their manes, the Festival of Joy began.

# 42

## *Sunday, December 14th*

On Sunday morning, the church basement was filled with the tantalizing aroma of blueberry pancakes.

The weekend had been a rousing success with everyone from Branscombe participating in the Festival—everyone except Betty and Jed, that is. With kidnapping and intent to murder charges pending, they would not be attending any candlelight ceremonies or pancake breakfasts for years to come.

Rufus Blackstone had taken three curtain calls when "A Christmas Carol" ended. Nora's story hour with the children had been standing room only, bringing out not only the kids, but the kids at heart. The lottery winners had all pitched in at Conklin's to help cater the Festival, Sam and Marion working side by side all weekend.

At the table where Alvirah and Willy, Regan and Jack, Nora and Luke, Muffy and Steve, Duncan and Flower, and

Duncan's fellow lottery winners were seated, they were all exultant.

"I hope they don't throw the book at the Winthrops," Flower said. "They *did* try to save me and almost lost their lives because of it."

"The one I feel sorry for is their Aunt Millie," Duncan said. "When she showed up here the other night to get the ticket from me, she almost fainted when she saw the cops and they told her that her nephews were in jail. Then when she tried to describe the convenience store where she supposedly bought the ticket, it was classic. I wish I'd had a camera with me." He laughed. "She said it was on a busy street and she couldn't remember whether there was a gas pump out front or not. When I handed that ticket over to the police, I think they were stunned. It'll be interesting to see what happens with it."

"A judge will rule on that," Jack explained. "Those two crooks were on parole and shouldn't have been gambling. Who knows what the judge will decide?"

"I just can't believe that I never suspected Betty Elkins of being so evil," Glenda said, shaking her head. "Boy was I dumb."

"Glenda if you hadn't come running into The Hideaway like that," Regan said, "Betty and Jed would have been on their way to that lake with Flower, and it might have been too late to stop them."

Duncan squeezed Flower's hand, then looked around

the table. "I can't tell you how grateful Flower and I are to all of you." He started to get choked up.

Flower smiled at him then looked at Alvirah. "It was so sweet of your friend Mrs. O'Keefe to offer to let us have the ring Duncan chose for me."

"She meant it but was thrilled when you turned her down," Alvirah laughed.

"Mr. Pettie is going to make a special flower ring for us," Duncan said. "I admit that I was really angry that he put the ring in the window, but if he hadn't—"

He didn't finish the sentence.

"We're going to get married on St. John's Island at the end of January," Flower said. "We want you and your families to be our guests for a long weekend at the resort there."

"We can make it," Willy said emphatically.

"We all can!" Tommy agreed.

# 43

*Friday, January 30th*

Six weeks later, Duncan fresh out of his cast, the whole group was sunning themselves on the beach the day before the wedding. Glenda's cell phone rang. She looked at the caller ID. "It's Harvey!" she said, exasperated. "Why won't he just leave me alone?" She answered. "What now, Harvey?"

"Glenda," he cried. "I just heard the judge's ruling on that other lottery ticket. He said it was null and void since those crooks had no right to buy it in the first place."

"I'm glad about that," Glenda said. "I've got to go."

"Wait! He also ruled that there was only one winning ticket. You people are going to get the whole pot!"

"The whole pot?" Glenda gasped.

"Twenty-four million each!" Harvey's voice cracked. "Glenda, we had a good thing going . . . We just hit a bump in the road . . ."

"Harvey, you've *got* to be kidding! I'll tell you what. I'll make a donation in your name to the BUZ network's

225

favorite cause." She hung up. The others were looking at her expectantly. "The judge has ruled that our ticket takes the whole pot!" she screamed. "The whole 360 million!"

Whoops and hollers could be heard the length of the beach. Tommy's mother jumped out of her chair. Ralph and Judy's daughters went running into the surf and began splashing each other. Marion and Sam looked stunned. "That's a lot of jelly donuts," Sam said. Duncan and Flower just smiled. At this point, another twelve million more or less didn't mean that much to them.

Regan, Jack, Nora, Luke, Muffy, and Steve just looked at each other.

"And I thought I was 'doing nice,' " Nora laughed.

Alvirah leaned forward. "This is all wonderful. But you must remember that much is expected of those to whom much has been given."

"Alvirah, don't worry. We're all planning to give to charity," Ralph assured her.

"That's good. And now, more than ever, I must insist you become members of my Lottery Winners Support Group. . . ."

Jack turned to Regan, his right eyebrow raised. "That's one group I wouldn't mind being asked to join."